"What happened to your first marriage, Leo?"

Teri needed to know why he had kept his distance from her, limiting their relationship to brief times of mutual enjoyment with no promises asked or given.

"After stringing me along for three years and conning me into buying a luxury family home, my cheating ex-wife finally told me she didn't intend to have children. Not my child or anyone else's."

His child!

The importance of her pregnancy to him was suddenly heart-sickeningly clear. She was having the child his wife had cheated him out of, and if he had to marry her to ensure his paternal rights to his son or daughter, that was what he was going to do!

Relax and enjoy our fabulous series of stories
about spirited women and gorgeous men, whose
passion results in pregnancies...sometimes
unexpected! Of course, the birth of a baby is
always a joyful event, and we can guarantee that
our characters will become besotted moms and
dads—but what happened in those nine
months before?

Share the surprises, emotions, dramas and
suspense as our parents-to-be come to terms
with the prospect of bringing a new little life into
the world.... All will discover that the business of
making babies brings with it the most special
love of all....

Look out next month for:
Having His Babies (#2057)
by Lindsay Armstrong

EMMA DARCY

Having Leo's Child

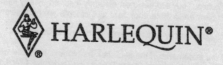

TORONTO • NEW YORK • LONDON
AMSTERDAM • PARIS • SYDNEY • HAMBURG
STOCKHOLM • ATHENS • TOKYO • MILAN • MADRID
PRAGUE • WARSAW • BUDAPEST • AUCKLAND

ISBN 0-373-12050-8

HAVING LEO'S CHILD

First North American Publication 1999.

Copyright © 1999 by Emma Darcy.

This edition published by arrangement with Harlequin Books S.A.

Visit us at www.romance.net

Printed in U.S.A.

CHAPTER ONE

NEVER had Teri Adams known such all-consuming sexual excitement. It amazed her, thrilled her, and she didn't care that she barely knew Leo Kingston.

He *wanted* her—this incredible, dynamic, beautiful, sexy man—and she hadn't known what *wanting* really felt like until he'd evoked it in her the very first time he'd walked into her restaurant. Instantly. Shatteringly. It was as though her body just lit up with new fields of awareness, prompting reactions and responses she had no control over. None at all.

The same thing happened the second time.

And this...the third...

She had to know it all, wanted to feel everything he could make her feel. If it was only this once...

There was nothing to hold her back. Everyone was gone; the customers, the chef, the kitchenhand. No one left to bother about, except herself and the man who'd stayed on, wanting to be with her, wanting *this* as madly and urgently as she did. From the moment he'd come in, ostensibly to buy his dinner, she'd felt it. This was going to be the night. He was going to act, going to reach out and pursue what was sizzling between them. And he had.

Her mouth was throbbing from the wildly erotic passion of his kiss. Her head was throbbing from the sheer volume of sensation it was trying to encompass.

Her heart was pounding like some madly beaten primitive drum. Her legs were a quivery mess, so much
so, in her rush to lead Leo to her bedroom above the
restaurant, she tripped on stairs she had never tripped
on before.

Leo, hard on her heels, saved her from falling, one
strong arm swooping around her waist, holding her
up, the other swiftly hooking her thighs, and she was
hoisted against his chest with barely a pause in his
forward momentum. On up the rest of the stairs he
carried her, the pumping excitement increasing at this
evidence of his power and strength.

With her arms flung over his shoulders and around
his neck, her breasts squashed to the heaving wall of
his chest, Teri dizzily absorbed the heat and the smell
of him, a vibrant male earthiness that her fevered
imagination attached to primitive instincts aroused
and raging. Without even realising what she was doing she licked along the line of his jaw, compelled to
taste, to saturate all her senses with him.

"Which door?" Leo growled.

"First one," she almost sang out of sheer exhilar-
ation, revelling in the wildness of being carried off
for mating by a caveman. Except Leo was clean-
shaven and the taste of him was like champagne fizz-
ing on her tongue and through her bloodstream. A
modern caveman, wanting, reaching out and taking,
and she loved it, loved being taken by *him*.

"Here?"

"Yes."

He kicked the door she'd left ajar, clearing their
passageway, and whirled her into the bedroom. She

expected him to crash onto the bed with her but he didn't, halting beside it and releasing her legs so they swung down to hang against his, and he caught her there while her arms were still wound around his neck, his hands clutching her bottom, squeezing her into a highly erotic knowledge of how powerfully excited he was.

He arched back, emitting an animal groan of pleasure as he revelled in the soft giving of her flesh. "You have the sexiest derrière I've ever seen on a woman, Teri," he declared. "And watching it twitch and sway under that snug little red skirt as you move around the tables in the restaurant..."

He dragged in a deep breath and it blew through her hair as his chin came down. Even in the semi-darkness his eyes had a mesmerising brilliance, cobalt-blue, glittering with the fully released fire of desire. "I tell you it's a diabolical tease," he went on, his voice furred with the lust she'd inspired. "My hands have been itching to hold you like this."

Her hands had been itching to touch any part of him, and if he had to talk about derrières, what his did to a pair of jeans was enough to make any woman start fantasising about taut and terrific flesh and muscle. Masculinity plus. And he was like that all over. But she contented herself with raking her hands through the lustrous black waves of his thick, springy hair as he kissed her again.

No one had ever kissed her like this. It wasn't a hard mash of his mouth against hers. It wasn't sloppy. It was a feast of sensation, his lips seductively shaping hers to be tantalised by little nips of his teeth and tingling caresses of his tongue, building excitement, then driving into an incredibly intimate sweep of her palate, electrifying every nerve-end, drawing her into a wild exchange of darting movements that brought such an intense rush of wanting, her whole body surged with need, demanding a carnal satisfaction that was shocking in its intensity.

"Phew! You've got me so steamed..." Leo gabbled gruffly as he lowered her onto her feet and eased back a bit. "...and I've barely started on all I've been aching to do."

Aching...yes...it felt as though every bone in her body was aching. She wasn't sure they were going to hold together.

He grinned a wild, wicked grin. "You know this smile printed on the red heart logo of your T-shirt? If you extend the curve upwards on either side..." He drew it with his two index fingers. "See? It goes directly to the peaks of your breasts. Beautiful geometry. Beautiful breasts..."

He circled her aureoles with his fingers, arousing acute excitement. "They're so perky and lush," he said huskily, his gaze dropping as he pulled her T-shirt from the waistband of her skirt and lifted it up...up...untangling her arms from his neck, tossing the garment aside, unfastening her bra, sliding the straps away. Then his hands were cupping her, his thumbs fanning her erect nipples and she could hardly breathe, so sharp was the pleasure of it.

The urge to touch him as he was touching her compelled her own hands to the buttons on his shirt, fingers travelling rapidly, parting the fabric, and his skin was as smooth as satin, hairless, tightly stretched over strongly delineated muscles. He felt wonderful, almost as though his skin was polished and her hands skimmed over him with sensual delight, amazed that a man could feel like this.

Wayne hadn't. But she instantly banished the memory of her ex-husband, long gone. There was no comparison to Leo. How could there be? This man was perfection.

In sheer fascination with him she rolled her thumbs over his nipples. He inhaled sharply, his chest expanding, seeming to pulse at the teasing touch, and a thrill of power zinged through Teri. The sure knowledge that she could and did affect him in the same way he affected her was intoxicating.

"Yessss," he hissed. "More…"

She slid the shirt from his shoulders and they were perfect, too, broad and strong and manly without being overly musclebound. While her hands revelled in gliding over the hard male curves of his upper arms, Leo freed himself of the constricting sleeves and hauled her close again, rubbing his bare chest against the soft mounds of her breasts, sensitising them further as he unbuttoned and unzipped her skirt.

It was so incredibly erotic…her flesh against his. She couldn't wait to feel the rest of him. Neither could he, scooping the rest of her clothes down, tearing his jeans apart, stepping out of them, shoes flicked off. Then there was nothing between them and they were free to embrace the totality of each other, skin against skin, exploring the differences with gloriously sensual and uninhibited fervor.

"You truly are...all woman," Leo said in a kind of awe that made Teri feel really special.

Though he was more so...everything she'd imagined he would be...complete and utter male power, sleek and strong and sure in his aggression, wanting her, revelling in her femininity, every taste and touch comprising a constant drive for more and more satisfaction in knowing her, all of her, and Teri could feel herself dissolving inside, like ice-cream subjected to heat, a thick flow of melting ice-cream, and he laid her on the bed and licked her as though he knew it and loved it and couldn't get enough of it, right down to every possible delicious drop.

Her mouth, her breasts, her stomach, and lower, parting her legs, moving to the most intimate folds of her and she was utterly helpless, her whole body focused on what he was doing to her, enthralled by the exquisite excitement of it...Wayne had never...but Leo...dear heaven! She closed her eyes and gave herself up to the pulsing ecstasy he was stoking with irresistible power.

And then his hand was touching her, too, cupping her, his thumb reaching into her, caressing, causing her to convulse with incredible pleasure, then sliding out to give way to his mouth...*his mouth!*...and she writhed to the terrible, wonderful madness of it, out of control, caught in the grip of sensations that simply rolled over any caring of what was done or how it was done as long as it kept going.

She cried out when it stopped, the need for continuance screaming through her. Her eyes flew open in urgent pleading. Her arms were limp, heavy, but she

lifted them, compelled to hold, to urge more from
him. But he was already coming to her, his knees
between her legs, and he was hastily sheathing himself with protection.

Shock momentarily slammed through her mind.
She hadn't thought…no matter…he had. It was all
right. And seeing him readying himself for her, the
brief cautionary cloud was instantly dispersed with a
ringing chant of yes…yes…yes…all of him inside
her…now, fast, hard, full-on, pounding as wildly as
her heart.

He slid an arm underneath her, lifting, and her body
instinctively arched to meet and welcome him, crav-
ing fulfilment of the promise, quivering with anticipation. She felt him slide into place, felt herself opening for him, wider and wider to accommodate his
wonderfully solid fullness and she almost died of
sheer delight as he pushed forward to the inner centre
of her being.

If he'd stopped then, Teri would have been content,
swimming in a sea of ecstasy. As it was, he paused
long enough to gather her up and kiss her, heightening
the sense of mutual possession, of melding with each
other, arousing levels of awareness that exulted in the
unifying force of this intense, physical mingling.

Stirred by the flow of his strength, Teri wound her
arms and legs around him and he took her with him
on a tumultuous ride that broke every barrier of experience she'd known until now. She was swamped
with roll after roll of exquisitely sweet sensation as
he immersed her in the beat of his mating, the powerful pacing of it pounding through her, consuming

every bit of sexual knowledge from her marriage and imprinting a new encyclopaedia of sensory perceptions, all of them measuring far beyond the realities she'd accepted before this.

Not that Teri was actively recording anything. It was simply happening to her. Leo was making it happen... Leo Kingston...and never in a million years was she going to forget how it was with him. And even when he climaxed he didn't let her go, didn't let the pulse of excitement seep away. He cuddled her, stroked her, kissed her, murmured what he wanted from her, guiding, and she abandoned herself to following his lead, revelling in his encouragement, his fierce responses, the supreme sensuality he drew from her.

How many times they coupled, how many ways... Teri had no idea. Leo seemed to know endless paths of pleasure though no matter how aroused he was, there was always care for unwelcome consequences, always another sheath of protection against their wild excesses, allowing absolute freedom to indulge themselves wherever desire took them.

There was no ultimate time of satiation, though eventually exhaustion did drug them into languorous periods of sleep from which they stirred when the entanglement of their bodies inadvertently caused movement and another awakening. The hunger for what they gave each other never abated. Even when dawn came they found a new fascination in making love in the softly filtered light, seeing, watching, gloating over their visual discoveries.

Leo's vivid blue eyes caressed her with warm pleasure as he trailed his fingertips around her breasts in deliciously teasing circles. He was hitched onto his side, one hand propping up his head, and his face wore a relaxed, happy expression. Such a handsome face, Teri thought, though it was really more than handsome.

His black eyebrows had a wicked arch to them, making his eyes a riveting feature. His nose was strong and straight, with a slight flare to his nostrils that drew attention to a mouth any woman would envy, lips that were sharply defined, sensually curved, and perfectly balanced. These attractions were heightened by an innate stamp of authority, an aura of self-confidence that said his thirty-something years had not been wasted. This was a man who went after what he wanted and got it.

She didn't match him in looks. Her hair was dark but hardly spectacular, cropped short for convenience. She liked her eyes best. They were large, light grey, with reasonably long lashes to emphasise them. Her nose, slightly tilted at the end, was invariably labelled cute. Her mouth was a touch wide and her lower lip was too full for Teri's liking.

She was certainly not strikingly beautiful but she was passably attractive and there was nothing wrong with her figure. In actual fact, there was a lot right with her figure. Ever since her teens it had drawn attention from the opposite sex, but she'd been with Wayne most of her life, so such attention was irrelevant. She wasn't interested. She was even less interested after her marriage had failed. A body was simply functional. That was all. Until Leo.

He smiled at her, a slow, lazy, satisfied smile. "Feeling good?"

"Mmmh..." She felt like the proverbial cat who'd fed gluttonously on cream.

"So am I. Better than I've felt for a long, long time. You're a marvel to me, Teri."

She smiled, thinking all the marvels came from him. "The same for me, Leo."

"The thing is..." he started, then gave vent to a long sigh, withdrawing his touch which was a chillingly obvious sign of separation from her.

Teri instantly had the sense this was decision time. Morning had come. Where to next? Nerves that had been beautifully lulled, started twitching with apprehension. However physically intimate they'd been, Leo was virtually a stranger. He'd come prepared for sex. Did he make a practice of one-night stands?

His mouth tilted in apologetic irony. "I don't want to mislead you..."

She tensed, preparing herself for the worst-case scenario. Leo Kingston had given her something very special so she had nothing to complain about, even if it was to be only a one-off experience. Yet she couldn't help hoping this was the start of something more with him.

"...I love what we've been sharing..." he went on, his voice projecting strongly positive appreciation.

But... her mind supplied as her heart cramped. This was surely the carrot ahead of the stick. All along she had assessed him as too good for her, a high-flyer with class stamped all over him, which was why it was so amazing he'd wanted her, a working-class girl in a service industry. Silly to have any expectations of a deep and meaningful relationship.

"...but I'm not into marriage, Teri. I've been there, done that, and it wasn't good."

Marriage! She hadn't given a thought to any such future possibility. Now...with him...had completely dominated her mind.

"You're divorced?" she asked. Although he had declared himself *a guy on his own* the last time he was here, Teri wanted to know if his wife was still around.

"Very much so," he answered sardonically.

"So am I," she confessed. "No fun, is it?"

"None whatsoever."

"So what are you saying, Leo? You'd like an affair with me as long as I understand wedding bells are out?" she prompted, hoping she had the affair part right.

That idea didn't upset her at all. *If* he was considering it. And she appreciated his honesty in warning her off any marriage aspirations. It was best to know where one stood. With Wayne, the sorting through where both of them wanted to go had been long and painful and the sense of failure a deep and scarring torment.

"Are you okay with that, Teri?" Leo asked, searching her eyes very seriously.

She wondered what scars he carried from his marriage. Needing some insight into where he was coming from, she asked, "Why don't you spell out what you do want, Leo?"

His face lit with an irrepressible grin. "What we've

just had. Over and over again. As long as it's good
for us.''

Her heart kicked with a wild surge of happy relief.
She wanted that, too, as many times as he'd give it
to her. Having lived twenty-nine years without ex-
periencing half of what Leo had touched off in her,
she'd be mad to pass up the opportunity to feel all
this again. Nevertheless, he hadn't told her much.
Only that their pleasure was mutual, which she already knew.

"So we're talking strictly sex, are we?" she lightly
probed, careful not to scare him off.

He frowned, clearly cogitating the equation he
wanted. "That sounds rather bald," he said slowly.
"I like you, Teri. Very much. And I don't want to
offend you."

"Honesty won't offend me, Leo," she assured him.
"I'd appreciate not being fooled in any way whatsoever."

God knew she'd fooled herself with rosy expectations going into her marriage with Wayne. She'd
sworn never to enter another relationship without pin-
ning everything down. Having her eyes wide open
and seeing straight left one a lot less susceptible to
miserable disappointment.

It had also narrowed the field of possible men she'd
accept in her life so drastically, Leo was the first
who'd passed the barriers she'd put up. Though he
hadn't precisely passed them. He'd burst through
them. Which made her all the more fascinated by him.
She studied his face—the self-knowing intelligence

and determination so evident on it—as he answered her.

"I simply don't want the kind of relationship that hangs a whole lot of emotional blackmail on either of us, Teri. I don't have the time or the stomach for it." A flash of bitterness there, almost instantly softened by an appealing, whimsical smile. "I guess I want things free and easy between us. Which is probably completely selfish..." He shrugged, not caring that it was. It was how he wanted it.

"You mean no accountability. Just take it as it comes," she interpreted.

He nodded. "I travel quite a bit in my business. I can be away for weeks at a time, so don't expect some kind of regular arrangement. It won't happen..." His eyes hardened. "...and I won't be pressured into it."

It was clear their affair would proceed on his terms or he'd call it quits. Teri wasn't sure how she felt about that...the total disregard for whatever needs she might have. Though he certainly fulfilled one need. He was top of the pack on that score. Absolutely top.

Her gaze glided down his magnificent physique and the lust for more of him gripped the pit of her stomach. No love involved here. Once she would have thought herself...sluttish...for feeling as she did now, but love had only brought her disillusionment. Why not take what she could get from this man? At least it was something good. Better than good. Fantastic!

She'd been working hard, establishing her restaurant business, virtually to the exclusion of everything else except visiting her family now and then. She'd earned a bit of spice in her life. Hot spice! She couldn't help grinning at the thought and her eyes danced back up to his.

"Okay," she agreed. "No commitments. Just when it suits both of us."

Relief and sparkling delight shone from him. "Great! You're a woman in a million, Teri. Finding you is like winning the lottery."

She laughed. "Maybe I got a bottle of champagne in you, Leo."

"Then celebration is in order," he said with a purposeful gleam.

He kissed her and the champagne fizzed so beautifully, Teri had no regrets over the bargain it sealed with Leo Kingston.

Pure pleasure.

No harm in that.

As long as she didn't attach anything else to it.

CHAPTER TWO

Ten months on...

PREGNANT!

No doubt left.

She was having Leo's child.

In the time it took to walk out of the clinic where the doctor had handed her the definitive test results, Teri managed to get her mind, which had been temporarily shattered by the positive confirmation of her suspicions, into relative working order. It moved from baby to birth to the reminder that today was her thirtieth birthday.

When she'd married Wayne, she'd imagined having two children by the time she was thirty, their own little family. She certainly hadn't imagined having a baby on her own, by a man who had no desire whatsoever to become her husband. So here she was, presented with two big milestones in her life, and a very different kind of future in front of her.

There was no question about what she was going to do. Fate might have thrown her a curve with this accidental pregnancy, but it might very well be the best thing that could ever happen to her. She would get to be a mother, which she didn't want to miss out on. There was no guarantee about how long Leo would stay in her life. Or any other man, for that

19

matter. A child was forever. Someone of her very own to love…without question…without limit.

Excitement at that thought welled and ebbed as she waited on the sidewalk for the traffic lights to change. Traffic roared up and down Oxford Street. Sydney was enjoying a brilliant summer and the late afternoon sunshine basked her in warmth. The fifteen-minute walk back to her restaurant in Paddington was an easy stroll and gave her time to recollect herself.

The red light changed to green and she pushed her legs into action, pushing her mind out of its fuzzy maternal wallow, as well. Single motherhood was not going to be easy. Maybe she was mad to take it on. But she couldn't bear not to. And one thing she could definitely say about Leo Kingston. He had fantastic genes.

If she'd actually been planning to have a baby without the support of a husband, and looking around for the best possible male specimen to supply the necessary, Leo would be a five-star choice…healthy, intelligent, good-looking, athletic, possessing the drive to get ahead in the world, and loaded with sex appeal.

How he'd react to being told he was going to be a father, Teri had no idea. Right at this moment, she didn't really care. She could do without spice…if she had to. A baby represented far more essential things to her.

Apart from finding her desirable, and companionable enough to enjoy chatting with her—occasionally—when it fitted into his business schedule—she didn't think Leo attached any importance to her role in his life. All his energy was poured into making his computer company more and more successful. Well, not quite all. When he focused his energy on bedding her, Teri still found it an irresistible force.

But he didn't even know it was her birthday today. Maybe over the past ten months she should have tried to make more of their relationship, though her experience with her ex-husband had taught her that pressing for anything would get her nowhere. Impossible to force what didn't come naturally. Leo had set the limits. *He* hadn't tried to change them, which surely meant he hadn't wanted to.

However, it was one thing to be free and easy lovers.

Parenthood was an even more permanent tie than marriage!

Having arrived back at her restaurant, Teri paused to view its street frontage, feeling a sense of pride in what she had achieved here. The idea of selling meals by weight had really taken off. Patrons could pile as much or as little as they liked on their plates and the price they paid for it was commensurate with how much they chose.

It was perceived as an exceptionally fair deal, the food was tasty, and Teri knew she had a lot of satisfied customers because they kept returning. In droves. Most lunches and dinners were sell-outs. It had become a nicely profitable little business. Nothing grand. But she could afford to employ a chef and a kitchenhand.

She didn't need financial support from Leo, should he choose to…not be around any more. She *was* capable of standing on her own two feet. Living in the apartment upstairs made the situation manageable. She would still be able to work and look after a baby.

As her gaze belatedly registered the name she'd given her restaurant, laughter gurgled up in her throat and spilled into a slightly hysterical peal. *Full Tummy—Happy Heart* was printed across the two front windows in a semicircular hump. A very pregnant hump, she thought in ironic amusement, and determined then and there, no matter how Leo reacted to her full tummy, she'd still have a happy heart about having his child.

She checked her watch as she pushed open the door. Four-thirty. The lull before the next onslaught of fast and furious activity. The tables were cleaned up and set for the evening meal.

Behind the weighing counter, Dylan, her chef, was busy cleaning up his open grill, ready for the dinner orders. Chunky, ginger-haired, freckle-faced, and invariably good-natured, he swung around as he heard her come in and shot her a cheerful grin.

"Leo called."

Teri's heart fluttered. Leo *never* called. Why today of all days? "What for?" she asked, hoping her voice sounded normal.

"Said he was flying in from New Zealand, and he'd be here about eight-thirty and if I was making that chicken mince stuff wrapped in spinach leaves, would I please keep him some?"

Food! Nothing personal. She heaved a sigh to get rid of the surge of absurd emotional hope for something different from Leo and aimed a smile at her chef. "Guess you made a hit with that dish, Dylan."

"Yeah."

He looked pleased. At twenty-two, he was still fresh from his long apprenticeship in a hotel and enjoying making his own little specialties.

"Mail came while you were out," he informed her, still grinning. "I put it in the kitchen."

"Thanks."

Probably birthday cards from her family, she thought, wondering how they were going to react to a new birth. Plenty of time before she'd have to tell them, but Leo...only four hours before he swept in, probably expecting two appetising meals. He'd get one. Then...

Well, it wouldn't be the end of the world if he dropped her flat. She'd coped fairly well after Wayne had walked out of their three-year marriage. She was used to being independent, working things out for herself, setting goals and reaching them for the most part.

At least this time, she wouldn't be left with nothing.

She was going to have a baby.

CHAPTER THREE

LEO KINGSTON was smiling as he strode out of the airport terminal and grabbed the first cab on the taxi rank. His business in New Zealand had been successfully concluded, the flight had landed on schedule, he was bound to get the kind of food he really enjoyed eating at Teri's restaurant—tasty but not too fancy, and a proper plateful instead of the skimpy servings the classy restaurants charged a fortune for—then to top off everything, a night of sheer, uncomplicated joy with Teri.

"Where to?" the driver asked.

"Jersey Road, Woollahra."

Home first to drop off his bags, have a quick shower, change into more casual and cooler clothes than his suit, a three-block walk which was just about right to get rid of the claustrophic feeling of plane travel, and he'd be at the door of *Full Tummy—Happy Heart.*

He grinned over the great name Teri had chosen for her restaurant. It was spot-on. Delivered precisely what it said. No pretensions. Just like Teri herself. He was really looking forward to being with her again. Great woman. She didn't nag, didn't sulk, never called him to account over anything, had no unreasonable expectations of him, made no demands,

24

didn't keep a clock on him, always enjoyed their times together, and she had a fantastic body.

It stirred him just thinking about the way Teri was built. She was so curvy and *female*. No bones sticking into him, just soft rounded flesh a man could really sink into and revel in. A real woman.

He remembered when he first saw her. Must be almost a year ago now. It was soon after he'd bought the terrace house in Jersey Road, when he'd been scouting the area for restaurants that provided good meals. Teri's place had been a great find. No waiting forever to be served, either, though he hadn't minded sitting over his dinner because just watching Teri had been a real pleasure.

He'd liked everything about her—the way she smiled at customers and cared about them being satisfied with what they'd chosen. Beautiful eyes. Touchable hair. An efficient manner without being abrupt. And a body that most women—in Leo's experience—would have traded on. But there wasn't even a hint of *The Princess Syndrome* in Teri Adams. Which made her even more attractive. And desirable.

He hated the be-my-slave-because-I'm-beautiful attitude a lot of women gave out. He'd had a gutful of it from his ex-wife, expecting him to dance attendance on her, provide her with everything her greedy little heart desired, pouting and carrying on when he had to put business first.

It would be a long time before he shackled himself to another marriage. If ever. He'd been so deceived by Serena, how the hell could a man know when a woman was pulling the wool over his eyes? Besides, freedom was good. He'd had three years of it since the parting of the ways with his self-serving ex-wife and he liked it better all the time.

Teri obviously appreciated her freedom, too. Nothing like a failed marriage to get you thinking about what you really wanted to do with your life. She was a smart businesswoman. The way she'd tapped into a highly marketable idea was truly admirable. He had a lot of respect for Teri Adams. She could stand on her own two feet and meet him on equal ground.

The cabbie turned into Jersey Road and Leo directed him to the home he'd made his own, which was nothing like the status symbol house Serena had insisted upon, undoubtedly with an eye to taking half the proceeds of its sale as her divorce price. This place was all his.

It was ten past eight when he walked into his living room and glanced around, gleaning pleasure from the familiar, comfortable layout he'd chosen for himself and feeling a deep sense of satisfaction in his independence.

The cleaner had been in, leaving everything shipshape. Didn't need a wife for that. There was his man-size leather chair and footstool with the coffee-table handy, placed directly in front of the maxi-screen television so he could watch his favourite sports in absolute comfort. No wife to complain about how much time he spent on it instead of sharing things with her—never mind her never trying to share things with him.

This was good. All it lacked was a woman in his bed. But the price of that was too damned high. And a wife didn't guarantee it, either. Sex was doled out at her convenience, not his, and only when he'd performed as he should in her eyes. Well, to hell with that!

Teri suited him just fine and he obviously suited her. Which reminded him to get moving. Shower, shave...full tummy, happy heart.

A very happy heart tonight!

CHAPTER FOUR

TERI checked her watch again—8:31. This *waiting* was dreadfully distracting, not to mention nerve-racking. So Leo was a minute late, she argued fiercely to herself. He might be half an hour late. He might not come at all. He hadn't *promised* anything. It was stupid to be working herself into a state with this constant clock-watching.

If Dylan had kept his mouth shut, she would have been sailing serenely through the evening, doing her job as she always did, without feeling as though she had a hive of buzzing bees inside her. In actual fact, she'd prefer it if Leo didn't turn up. Tomorrow night or any night in the future would be soon enough to tell him she was having his child. Then there'd be no possibility of feeling anything bad about going to bed alone on her thirtieth birthday.

Teri concentrated on counting notes out of the till. Most of her clientele were working people who didn't want to cook for themselves and they'd either been and gone home or were still eating. Nine-thirty was closing time. Which would fit nicely into giving a baby its night feed, she assured herself.

The doors whooshed open.

Teri's head jerked up.

Leo!

He came striding through the dining room, not

glancing at the buffet section where a tempting array of food was still laid out, paying no attention whatsoever to the people seated at the tables, what they were eating or doing or chatting about. The bright, red-check cotton tablecloths, the little bowls of daisies, the framed black-and-white cartoons of people feasting that she'd hung on the walls...none of them rated the slightest bit of notice.

Leo made straight for the weighing counter behind which Teri stood, exuding an energy that instantly had her heart zinging. His blue jeans and royal-blue sports shirt meant he was well and truly off work tonight and the twinkle in his blue eyes held an almost wicked glee in the freedom to do whatever he liked.

"Hi!" he said, leaning his arms on the top of the cash register and grinning at Teri, his handsome face radiating the strong power of a winning personality.

Teri tried to keep her feet on safe, sensible ground, despite her toes tingling. He had great teeth, she thought, white and straight, and somehow they combined with his eyes to deliver a charismatic impact that curled her insides and sent miniquakes down her legs. It would be good if their child inherited his teeth and eyes, Teri decided, trying valiantly to distance her mind from Leo's physical effect on her.

"Good trip?" she asked. Her mouth had a will of its own. It was smiling back at him. Or maybe Leo mesmerised her muscles into responding to the pleasure he was pouring out.

"Achieved what I wanted," he said with satisfaction. And he intended to do that here, too, his eyes said in no uncertain terms.

She was wearing the uniform she'd designed for the restaurant; a white T-shirt emblazoned with a red heart on which a simple white curve representing a smile had been painted, a neat little red skirt and comfortable white loafers on her feet. She could feel her breasts peaking into the soft fabric of the T-shirt and wished she had two red hearts positioned to disguise the fact.

"I can see success has put you in a good mood," she commented, intent on holding Leo's gaze on her face. If it drifted downwards the problem would surely worsen.

"Coming *here* puts me in a good mood," he replied, making the message very personal.

Maybe not after tonight, her mind clicked in, but her body didn't want to respond to that sobering piece of caution.

"Hey, Leo!" Dylan broke in, popping his head out of the kitchen. "I put four of the Changmai Surprise aside for you. I'll microwave them now if you like."

"Great!" Leo beamed at him. "And I'll follow them up with your lamb kebabs if they're on the menu."

"Will do," Dylan agreed cheerfully.

"That guy really knows what to do with food," Leo remarked as Dylan retreated into the kitchen. "You got a prize in him, Teri."

"Yes, I did. And every chef likes to have his creativity appreciated. It gave him a real buzz, your calling this afternoon."

He laughed. "Pure self-interest. The thought of

plane food did not appeal. Have you eaten yourself, yet?"

"Bits and pieces." Her stomach had been too screwed up to accept much.

His eyebrows slanted in charming appeal. "Join me at my table?"

She nodded. "When I've finished up."

He gave the remaining diners a quick scan. "Not too many left. Shouldn't take long." Another dazzling smile. "I've been looking forward to your company."

"You mean I rank up there with the food?" she lightly mocked, trying to quell the maverick rush of need to know how highly she did rank in his life.

His eyes danced, inviting her to be his partner in pleasure as he replied, "I have a hunger for many things."

"Mmmh..." she answered noncommittally.

"I'll do my best to tease your appetite," he promised.

And she'd probably rob him of his, Teri thought with savage irony. His black wavy hair was still damp from a shower. She could smell the tangy cologne he'd splashed on his newly shaven jaw. He was certainly primed for sexual action, and the mental picture formed of Leo stripped naked, his powerful masculinity all hers for the night...if she postponed telling him about her pregnancy.

The temptation to keep that vital piece of news to herself was suddenly very strong. Leo might value freedom above everything else but he was a great lover. Why deprive herself of one more sensational experience with him? She could look upon it as a birthday gift to herself.

"Teri?" Leo quizzed her silence.

Her mouth twitched. "Just thinking how good you look, Leo."

He grinned. "You, too, babe."

Babe!

She should be thinking of what was between his ears, not his legs. Even more pertinently what was in his heart! Would being a father *mean* anything to him?

"Here you go, Leo!" Dylan announced, sliding the plate with its steaming appetiser straight onto the weighing machine beside the cash register.

Leo sniffed appreciatively. "Love that sauce, Dylan."

"Combination of honey, sesame oil and soy sauce," Dylan confided proudly.

Teri took the printout of the weight, stapled on a customer number, gave the matching number to Leo, then spiked the bill for later payment. "Enjoy," she said with an encouraging smile.

"Back soon," he warned both of them and headed for his usual table against the wall from where he could watch all the action.

Dylan set to work grilling the lamb kebabs and Teri did the rounds of the tables, removing used plates while having a bit of chitchat with regulars. She was acutely conscious of Leo's eyes following her. It was almost like the caressing touch of his hands, shaping her body to his, or that was how it felt to her fevered imagination. His close presence made her so sexually aware, she escaped to the kitchen to sort herself out on some kind of sensible level.

"I'll do those." Mel Hudson, her kitchenhand, who was working his way through university, whipped the tray of dirty plates out of her hands. "You go and enjoy yourself with Leo." And the nineteen-year-old lanky boy winked at her!

Teri huffed and muttered, "He'll keep."

Mel proceeded to load the dishwasher, a knowing grin on his face. "The guy's on toast for you, Teri. You ought to put him out of his misery."

"When I want your advice, Mel,"—cheeky "I'll ask for it."

s your birthday. Give yourself a break."

frowned at him. "Who told you it was my rthday?"

"Dylan figured it had to be. The post came when you were out this afternoon and he said there was a whole stack of cards for you."

Which she'd taken upstairs to the apartment, out of sight, out of mind. Of course, her family meant well, but what woman wanted to be reminded of her thirtieth birthday? "Some people ought to mind their own business," she remarked darkly.

Mel shrugged. "So what's the big deal? Take the rest of the night off. Have fun. Dylan and I will finish up and shut up shop."

"I'm not ready," she muttered truculently.

"Ready for what?"

"Never you mind."

She banged some pots and pans around to indicate the conversation was over. Her mind chewed over her

state of readiness. Was she ready to go to bed with
Leo with him still in ignorance of his fatherhood?
Ready to tell him she was pregnant? Ready to suffer
his shock, dismay, rejection? This was extremely difficult to sort out.

She liked the man. She liked having him in her life,
even if it was on a casual basis. In fact, if she was
still a starry-eyed teenager she'd probably say she was
in love with Leo Kingston, though from a more ma-
ture outlook, that was probably only chemistry. After
all, she didn't know him through and through. Only
that he was nice to people, nice to her, fun to be with,
and great in bed.

Both Dylan and Mel liked him but that was a
to-man thing. Leo, in their opinion, was a good
However, not one of them had any *claim* on him.
breezed in and out and he was much more out than
in. Even so, was she really ready to say goodbye to
him?

She'd been able to think much more clearly this
afternoon. Somehow, Leo's being here, hitting her
with so much vital attraction again, completely muddled her.

"Teri...customer leaving," Dylan called out.

She hastily pasted a smile on her face and went to
handle the departing customer's payment for dinner.
Leo was at the serving counter and Dylan was transferring the lamb kebabs from the grill to a plate that
was already piled up with various salads chosen from
the buffet table. Teri managed the money transaction
smoothly, bade good-night to the family of four who
appeared well satisfied, then went through the routine
of weighing Leo's main meal.

"Join me now?" he pressed hopefully.

"Sure she can," Dylan popped in. "The grill's off for the night so I can handle the cash takings and Mel will do the rest."

A birthday conspiracy, Teri concluded, which was really nice, but not exactly timely when she wasn't ready for the outcome. "Something I've got to do upstairs first," she quickly excused. "Sure you don't mind filling in for me, Dylan?"

He grinned. "Piece of cake."

"You look perfect as you are," Leo remarked warmly, his eyes more than warm. The fire of desire was well and truly kindled.

She gave him a droll look. "If you think I'm going to titivate for you..."

He laughed. "That's what I love about you, Teri. Always *au naturel*."

"Hmmph," she said, and feeling a blush coming on, made a swift exit.

Love...she ruminated frenziedly over that as she headed upstairs. It was most probably a throwaway word, she argued, like Leo saying he *loved* Dylan's sauce. He couldn't mean he actually *loved* her.

Was real love ever held at the kind of distance Leo kept? Not in Teri's understanding of it. However, tagged on to the *au naturel* remark, it made sense. Oh yes! No doubt about how much he loved tangling with her naked.

And she loved tangling with him naked!

Which was what was making everything so difficult.

She reached her small and rather cluttered living room and raced over to the mantelpiece where she'd lined up her birthday cards. If...if she invited Leo upstairs tonight, she didn't want him to see them, didn't want him asking how old she was or bringing out the telling fact that neither of them knew each other's birthdays.

She bundled them up and was about to shove them into the drawer of her writing desk, when the one on top caused her to pause. It was the big pink flowery one from her parents with the gold inscription—*To Our Darling Daughter.*

A daughter…

She hadn't thought past…baby. Even a baby wasn't quite real to her yet, not enough to put either sex to it. A daughter…or a son…her heart turned over.

Slowly, she laid the cards in the drawer and slid it shut. Then she turned around and leaned back against the desk, her hands creeping up to spread across her flat stomach. As flat as it was, a baby was somewhere in there growing…a little girl or boy…her child…Leo's child.

She had to tell him.

And it had to be done tonight.

Impossible to make love with this huge secret swimming around in her mind, Leo touching her where their child was actually forming, not knowing about it.

The decision was very clear.

She was ready now…ready to tell Leo she was having his child.

CHAPTER FIVE

IT STARTLED Teri to see the dining room almost empty when she returned. There were only two couples left, eating their choice of sweets. Dylan was cleaning the grill and Mel was chatting with Leo who'd obviously finished his main course since Mel had cleared his table. A glance at her watch showed 9:15. Time had flown since Leo had arrived.

"Ah, here you are!" Mel said with satisfaction, and held out the chair opposite Leo's for her.

"Thanks," she said, her eyes quizzing this unanticipated gesture of gallantry from her teenage employee.

Mel grinned. "No problem. Leave you to it now."

Teri rolled her eyes to Leo who looked most amused at this little byplay. "Why do I feel I'm being pushed at you tonight? Are they up to no good behind my back?" she dryly remarked.

He laughed, his eyes twinkling like brilliant sunshine on blue water. "They like you, Teri. They like working for you. You make this a good place to be. They want to give you some time off. That's all."

She sighed. Leo really was a gorgeous man. "You know you've never told me how many people work for you."

He had explained his business as software conversions, but Teri hadn't probed much, not wanting Leo to think she was interested in how big his income was. That didn't matter to her. However, she needed a safe, impersonal kind of conversation until they were absolutely alone together.

He shrugged. "Small team. Four crack computer programmers and one administrative assistant."

"Any females?"

"The assistant." He gave a crooked little smile. "Mavis is in her early fifties, frighteningly efficient while sort of mother-henning the rest of us."

She hadn't been checking out possible female competition, but it was interesting to know the kind of woman he'd hired. "Do you prefer your programmers to be men?" she asked, aware there were many women in computer fields these days.

Something negative flicked across his face. "It's easier," he said flatly.

"How so?" she asked curiously.

He sighed. "You'll probably accuse me of being some kind of male chauvinist, but the truth is most whiz-bang computer programmers are fairly young and a lot of young women trade off their sex appeal." An icy hardness flashed into his eyes. "They can bring tensions into a workplace I simply don't want. Guys start competing for their attention and an atmosphere of camaraderie is suddenly shot to pieces. It's just better avoided."

"You've seen this happen?" Teri asked, uneasy with his explanation which did smack of male bias.

He nodded. "Married women are usually okay but unmarried ones can play havoc with productivity and team spirit."

So it wasn't exactly a bias against women, more a pragmatic choice to guard against hormone battles. But he certainly didn't care for women who traded on their sex appeal. Teri couldn't help wondering what his ex-wife had been like. They'd never swapped marriage stories. Raking over that particular part of her past had not appealed to her. Still didn't. And she didn't have the right to poke into his.

Besides, even the mention of marriage might be misinterpreted when she had the highly sensitive subject of her pregnancy waiting in the wings.

She smiled. "I guess you consider Mavis safe."

He relaxed and returned her smile, pleased she wasn't critical of his employment policy. "Absolutely safe. Mavis is great. Reliable, responsible, has a place for everything and everything in its place."

Teri wondered if Leo applied some of those headings to herself...like *safe* and *in her place*. She certainly didn't constitute a distraction from his work. She suspected she was his break from it.

The big question was...how would he view a baby?

The shifting of chairs alerted her to the imminent departure of the remaining diners. She glanced around. Yes, all of them up, ready to go. Dylan was at the cash register, waiting to take their money. Mel had cleared the buffet table and was hurrying out of the kitchen to clean up the tables being vacated.

"Do you want dessert, Leo?" Teri asked, swinging her attention back to him. There'd still be leftovers in the kitchen.

He gave her a whimsical look. "It's being taken care of."

She raised her eyebrows. "More special service?"

"I think I've won special status by winning your favour."

"Leo, I suspect you'd win any woman's favour if you worked on it." And that was the plain truth, Teri thought.

"You miss the point," he argued, his eyes dancing at her again. "It's you who's special, Teri."

How special? Was he prepared to accept her as the mother of his child?

"Well, thanks," she said as graciously as she could manage when her nerves were getting strung out like piano wires. "It's nice to be appreciated."

"Oh, you are! Very much," Leo asserted, desire flowing from him in electric waves that instantly screwed the piano pegs up another notch or two and caused her stomach to go into spasms.

Fortunately Dylan provided distraction, escorting the last of tonight's customers to the door and locking up behind them. "You and Mel can go, too, Dylan," Teri instructed. "If there's anything left to do, I'll do it in the morning."

"Okay. We'll be off in a minute. Just got to hang up my apron," Dylan returned cheerfully.

One more minute and she could start unburdening herself of this dreadful suspense. A sixty-seconds countdown to desertion or togetherness or a continuation of their *sometime* relationship into *sometime* fatherhood. And the strange part was, Teri had no idea which outcome would be best in the long run.

"Is something wrong, Teri?" Leo asked.

It forced her to meet the quizzical concern in his

eyes. "Not really," she answered, wishing the boys would hurry up.

"You look a bit strained."

"Sorry." She tried a rueful smile. "There's nothing wrong." An innocent baby on the way could hardly be called *wrong*. "It's just...well, I have a lot on my mind."

"Anything I can do to help?"

The offer was genuine. She could see nothing but sincerity in his expression. Maybe...

"Happy birthday to you..."

Dylan's and Mel's voices raised raucously in song, instantly jerked her attention away. Her two young employees were marching out of the kitchen, Dylan carrying a cake with a single candle burning on it, Mel bearing a tray with two flute glasses and a bottle of champagne in an ice bucket.

"Happy birthday to you..."

Leo rose from his chair to join in.

"Happy Birthday, dear Teri-i-i..."

They were all grinning like Cheshire cats.

"Happy birthday to you!"

She almost burst into tears. She quickly propped her elbows on the table and covered her face with her hands. Let them think she was embarrassed. Let them think anything as long as she had a few seconds to fight back this awful flood of turbulent emotion.

She heard the plate with the cake being plonked on the table in front of her. "Come on, Teri. Got to blow the candle out," Dylan cajoled.

"Make a wish, too," Mel pressed.

A wish...

Please God, let Leo want our child!

And why that suddenly meant so much she didn't know!

She took a deep breath, dropped her hands, and blew out the candle. It wasn't difficult to blow out one candle. If there'd been thirty...but they didn't know about that milestone and she wasn't about to tell them.

Her effort was roundly applauded.

"Thank you," she managed huskily.

"It's an orange cake with lemon icing. Your favourite. Made it myself," Dylan said proudly.

"You shouldn't..." She stopped herself from shaking her head and aimed a wobbly smile at him. "It's very kind of you, Dylan."

"Pleasure. You have a good time, Teri. Everyone should celebrate their birthday."

"Yeah," Mel agreed. "We're nicking off now so you can have a great celebration. Good night, Teri...Leo..."

"I'll lock up after you," Leo offered, and they all set off for the door, leaving Teri staring at a cake she couldn't possibly eat and a bottle of champagne that was utterly wasted on this occasion.

They meant well.

Any other birthday she would have been delighted at being given such a sweet surprise. She must thank Dylan and Mel again tomorrow. Her eyes misted over again and she blinked furiously, clearing the moisture as best she could. Getting choked up was not going to help anything. She took several deep breaths and was more or less in control of herself by the time Leo returned to the table.

Her hands fluttered in a dismissive appeal. "I didn't realise they had anything like this planned. I didn't even tell them it was my birthday."

"I know." He leaned down and picked something off his chair. "This is from me," he said, handing her a slim, rectangular packet, wrapped in expensive silver paper. "Happy birthday, Teri."

His voice was a warm caress, stroking her heart into pumping with the wild hope that ~~might not be the parting of the ways she fe~~ down at the packet as Leo slid back raised a host of questions that cla swered.

"How did you know, Leo?"

"Dylan told me when I rang this afternoon."

"He had no right..." A painful flush burned into her cheeks as she imagined Dylan suggesting to Leo that he surprise her, too. Her eyes flashed an anguished apology. "I didn't expect you to..."

He reached across the table and stilled the agitated wave of her hand by capturing it and pressing reassurance. "I wanted to, Teri. In fact, it's because you don't expect anything that it's a very real pleasure to buy you a gift."

"But..."

"No buts. Open it," he commanded softly, releasing her hand so she could do so.

She wavered, wanting to, yet not feeling right about it, not in these circumstances. "I don't even know *your* birthday," she temporised.

"First of December," he tossed off carelessly.

Their baby would be born in October.

She barely caught herself back from saying it. Too bald a statement. Better to lead into it so at least he understood how it had happened.

"It won't bite," Leo dryly advised. "And you won't owe me anything, Teri. It's simply a birthday gift, no strings attached. Please...I enjoyed buying it."

A child was a big, big string, Teri thought, as she tore open the wrapping paper, hoping Leo had picked up something simple and relatively inexpensive. He'd probably ducked into one of the airport shops and bought the first thing that caught his eye...except the long flat box emerging from the silver paper was a white leather case on which was stamped in gold, the high-fashion designer name—Escada.

Her heart wobbled as she clicked open the lid. Sunglasses—streamlined class—the elegant black-and-silver frames suggesting a space age design.

"Put them on and let me see," Leo urged, eager to judge if his choice was right.

Teri had never owned or worn a designer label *anything!* The temptation—just to try—was too seductive to deny. Her hands trembled slightly as she lifted the beautiful and undoubtedly ruinously expensive glasses from their black suede nest and fitted them on her face.

"Yes!" Leo cried triumphantly. "I knew they were *you* the moment I saw them. Take a look in the mirror, Teri. They look fantastic on you!"

She couldn't resist, just to see. A mirror was positioned on the wall so most of the dining room could be watched from the kitchen. It only took a few moments to get up and view her reflection. The sunglasses were wonderful; chic, classy, perfect for her face and cropped hair, giving her an ultra modern, sophisticated look that instantly took away any angst over being thirty.

She couldn't help smiling at Leo for giving her this lovely gift, despite the deep reservations she held. ''They are fantastic,'' she agreed wholeheartedly. ''But they must have cost a fortune, Leo.''

He shrugged, still grinning at her. ''Worth every cent. All you need now are black leathers and a Harley-Davidson.''

Laughter bubbled up from somewhere and spilled out. Teri tried to get a grip on herself as she resumed her seat at the table and returned the glasses to their plush case. She had to speak—*had to*—before she was drawn so far into Leo's charm-circle she'd want to forget the unforgettable.

''Time to open the champagne,'' he said happily.

''No...wait!'' she blurted out, halting his movement to lift the bottle out of the ice bucket. She met his quizzical eyes anxiously. ''There's something I've got to tell you, Leo.''

''Okay,'' he invited good-humouredly.

Where to start? How to start? Why hadn't she given this more thought?

''Remember last month when you were here and I had a bit of a queezy stomach?'' she plunged in, desperate to have him understand there'd been nothing planned about it.

He nodded. "The twenty-four-hour bug. I got it, too." He gave her a teasing smile. "Probably off you."

"Probably," she repeated. Her muscles had stiffened up. Impossible to return even a travesty of a smile. Get to the point, her mind screamed. Her voice obligingly recited, "Anyhow, I started vomiting after you left that night. And the doctor says that's why the pill didn't work."

Leo frowned as though he wasn't quite following her.

Teri took a deep breath. Obviously it had to be spelled out to him. Finding it too frightening to look him in the eye, Teri fastened her gaze on the snuffed-out candle on the cake and poured forth the truth.

"I'm pregnant, Leo. With your child. And I'm going to have it. Whether you like it not. So there you are. That's the situation." She heard herself babbling but couldn't stop. "I couldn't not tell you. Though I don't expect anything from you. I won't ask for anything, either. I want to have this baby. It's my decision. My responsibility. But I couldn't not let you know. It is your child."

The babble ran out.

Yet the words she'd said seemed to echo and echo in the long, long silence that followed, taunting her into finally looking up.

There was nothing coming from him.

Absolutely nothing.

Leo's face was frozen in shock.

CHAPTER SIX

PREGNANT...

Having his child...

Leo couldn't get it together in his mind. One level in his brain registered that the evening he'd planned with Teri was shot to pieces because this alien element had changed all the parameters. But the crux of everything revolved around...what was he supposed to do now?

He was floored. Knocked out for the count. And he seemed utterly incapable of picking himself up. He'd never got a woman pregnant before. He was careful about that. Responsible. He knew people were having babies when and as they liked these days, but he'd always thought if you were going to have kids, you did the right thing and got married first, set the process up properly.

And there was the sticking point.

He didn't want to get married.

He liked Teri. They had a good relationship going. At least, they had up until now. He didn't want it wrecked and there was nothing that wrecked a relationship faster than marriage. He'd already made one huge mistake with it and ended up paying one hell of a price for nothing.

But it wouldn't be nothing with Teri.

She was already pregnant with his child. A child

47

was definitely something. Though she hadn't meant
it to happen. It was clearly an accident. In fact, she
could have chosen to have an abortion, not telling him
at all.

A savage recoil hit his stomach. He was glad Teri
hadn't taken that path. Just the thought of her getting
rid of his child stirred up a prickly nest of primitive
instincts. He certainly had to hand it to her. She'd
done the decent thing, letting him know, giving him
the chance to...*be a father!*

His mind still boggled over being so unexpectedly
presented with a done deal. It was wrong somehow
that it should be an accident. Fatherhood was too important...a state to be approached with appropriate
planning and a readiness to take it on.

This haphazard situation represented a big compli-
cation to his current lifestyle. Teri's, too. Big...*big!*
They were looking at a responsibility that would
spread over the rest of their lives. Pregnancy...baby...child...teenager...a lot of years involved here...and a kid deserved parents who were
prepared to be parents and everything that meant.

He'd wanted a family before Serena had soured
him on the whole deal. Here it was being handed to
him. Well, not exactly a family. One child. A kid of
his own to show things to, share things with.

He remembered the great times he'd had with his
own Dad...camping, fishing, playing ball...the competition they'd had running for years, shooting balls
into the basketball hoop they'd fixed above the garage
door.

He was startled out of the pleasant memories by

Teri's pushing her chair back and standing up. Very abrupt it was, jarring, unexpected. They had serious business to discuss here and there couldn't be any running away from it.

He looked up to see her face was white and strained. Her grey eyes were oddly drained of colour, like a rain-washed sky, cold, dull and bleak.

"You don't have to worry about a thing, Leo. I leave you free and clear," she stated, a steely pride in her voice. "Don't forget to activate the lock on the door when you go."

With her head tossed high and a poker spine, she walked out on him, straight for the kitchen and undoubtedly heading for the privacy of her upstairs apartment.

Leo did nothing to stop her. If she'd slapped him in the face, he couldn't have been more stunned by the flat rejection she'd just handed him. He stared at the table, at the untouched cake, the uncorked champagne, the torn wrapping paper and the white leather case containing the *Escada* sunglasses. She hadn't even taken *them* with her...a gift he'd given in good faith.

Then he remembered how reluctant she'd been to join him at his table tonight, reluctant to open his gift. The words she'd spoken earlier came sliding back, gathering much more force...*I don't expect anything of you...I won't ask for anything...my decision...my responsibility.* It all added up to...Teri didn't want to share his child with him. She wanted to keep it to herself.

And damn it all! That wasn't right. He was the

father, wasn't he? It wasn't up to Teri to decide he could have no part of this. The kid was just as much a part of him as it was of her. That gave him a say in things, didn't it? He had a claim here, a flesh and blood claim, and he didn't want to be done out of it.

His mind moved into high gear, focusing strongly on the problem facing him. He could be on tricky legal ground with paternal rights. As a single Mum, Teri might be able to shut him out, or severely limit any fathering he might want to do.

Besides, going to a court of law rarely produced the best end result. A private settlement between the two parties was much better. In fact, his path was becoming very clear. He had to win Teri over to his way of thinking, show her he could be useful, supportive, worth having around when she needed help with the kid.

There had to be some way to sort things out. After all, the bottom line was Teri was having *his* child.

A child had the right to know its father.

That was a good line to take.

And what he had to do now was persuade Teri to accept it.

CHAPTER SEVEN

So, THAT was it, Teri told herself, staring numbly at the bed which she could have shared with Leo if she'd kept her mouth shut. She tried to banish the loneliness of the moment by sitting on it and ignoring the fact it was big enough for two. She'd need the extra room in it when she was heavily pregnant anyway.

She would have to go back downstairs soon, store the cake and champagne in the refrigerator, check that Leo had locked the door properly, and switch off the lights. No point in inviting a break-in. A thirty-year-old single mother had to be practical about the future.

She was on her own. No doubt about that now. She'd waited and waited for Leo to stop sitting on the fence and commit himself one way or another but he'd obviously found the situation too difficult to handle. After all, it was a bit crass to bluntly say, "I'm out of here," to a woman you've been bedding for a year, just because she'd fallen pregnant on a mischance.

And there really was nothing to gain by lying about how he felt being tied into fatherhood when she knew he didn't want permanent ties. Even if he'd manoeuvred for a few more nights of sex, the lie would be uncovered sooner or later and that would make him a sleazy rat.

At least she could take pride in letting him go with

51

grace and dignity on her part. Unfortunately pride didn't rate very highly at the moment. It didn't ease the ache in her heart. It didn't fill the awful emptiness of loss. It didn't stop her yearning for impossible things…like a man to love her, to stand by her regardless of what life threw at them, to be there for her when she really needed him.

Her long built-up defensive shield of self-sufficiency started cracking. She was only feeling these things because of the baby, Teri frantically reasoned, but tears began welling and it was hopeless trying to hold them back. Her eyelids couldn't contain them. They squeezed through her lashes and started trickling down her cheeks. She grabbed a handful of tissues from the box on the bedside table and did some mopping up, but the tightness in her chest needed some release and there was no one to care whether she wept or not.

The creaking of one of the old stair-treads jolted her into scooping in a deep breath. Had she imagined it? Her heart jumped as the creaking came again. It had to be the fourth and the ninth steps. Any weight on them and they…someone was coming up the staircase to her apartment!

"Teri?"

Leo!

He hadn't gone! He was still here…looking for her!

She held her breath and swiped wildly at the moisture on her cheeks as he moved down the hallway, past the open doorway to the blessedly dark bedroom, and on to the living room at the front of the house,

overlooking the street. The light there was still on
from her previous dash upstairs to put the birthday
cards away.

He didn't call out again, despite finding the room
empty of her presence. He probably figured she was
in the bathroom. She wished she *was* there so she
could wash her face. Though that wouldn't help the
rest of her. Her mind was totally flummoxed, trying
to find a motive for Leo's following her upstairs, and
her heart was catapulting around her chest. He
couldn't still expect—want—sex with her, could he?

She pushed up from the bed, sending a shot of
fierce willpower to her legs when they threatened to
give way. The shock had dried up her tears. She
dropped the damp tissues that had balled in her hand.
Whatever Leo's reasons for wanting to be with her,
there was no escape from confronting them.

Dignity, dignity, dignity, she recited to herself as
she left the bedroom and took the few steps down the
hallway to the doorway into the living room. Several
deep breaths helped restore composure, though her
pulse was still going nineteen to the dozen. The sight
of Leo calmly pouring champagne into one of the
flute glasses stopped her dead.

She stood absolutely still, watching him, curiously
mesmerised by the swift attack on her senses. He had
so much impact—his strong male physicality, the aura
of sublime confidence, the vital good looks—and this
was the father of her child. She was always going to
have a part of him.

Whatever else he could be labelled, Leo Kingston
was, undoubtedly, a champagne man. He had defi-

nitely put some quality fizz in her life and it was possible he would keep on doing it. After all, he was still here, wasn't he? Or maybe the fizz was about to go flat.

Once he'd filled the flute glass to his satisfaction, he set it down on the tray he'd obviously collected from the kitchen, and picked up the second glass, proceeding to do the same again. The tray, which he'd placed on the small table between her two armchairs, not only carried the ice bucket for the bottle of champagne, but the cake Dylan had made for her, and the single candle had been relit!

"What are you doing?" The inane question spilled from her lips. It was perfectly obvious he was pouring out champagne. She should have asked *why* he was doing it. And why the cake with the lit candle?

Leo instantly flashed a happy grin at her. "There you are!" he said, which was also obvious.

Happy? Teri's confusion grew as she felt Leo pouring positive vibrations at her. "I thought you…" She stopped herself from uttering another inanity. When a man was standing in front of her, he certainly wasn't gone.

He put down the bottle, picked up the filled glass from the tray, and carried it over to her, his grin projecting a veritable flood of pleasure. "I thought we should celebrate." He handed her a glass and clicked it with his. "A toast to you on your birthday, and a toast to our child whom I figure is one month along, which is just as good as a birthday so I lit the candle for both of you."

He sipped his drink with every appearance of rel-

ishing the words he'd just rattled out and Teri followed suit, too dazed to question the turnaround from
shock to celebration.

"When did you find out?" he burbled on. "About
the baby I mean." His eyes expressed keen interest.

"Today," she answered.

"Only today?" There was a flicker of concern.
"You're not going to change your mind about having
it?"

"No, I'm not," she said decisively, inwardly tens-
ing at the thought he hoped she might.

The concern cleared. "Right! Fine!"

His apparent relief and approval left her speechless.
She just didn't understand what Leo was about. Was
this an act to keep their relationship going for a
while? Had he reasoned out she wasn't in-your-face
pregnant yet, so he might as well ride along until
convenience became inconvenience?

His expression changed to apologetic appeal. "I
guess it took *you* some time to get used to the idea,
too."

Was that all it had been downstairs? Time frozen
as he groped towards getting used to the idea? Teri
still couldn't dismiss the sense of disbelief stirred by
his current behaviour.

"You don't mind about what's happened?" she
queried, her eyes keenly searching his for any dubious
signs.

"Do you?" he instantly countered, watching just
as acutely for her reactions.

"Well, it wasn't exactly planned..."

"No, I know," he came in quickly. "Bit of a shock

being told you're going to be a father when you're
not expecting it. Must have been a shock to you, as
well, being told you're going to be a mother.''

"Yes, it was," she conceded.

"But it's okay. I mean you really do want it."

He seemed quite anxious on that point.

"I would have preferred a more ideal situation,"
she said dryly. "Being a single mother does have its
drawbacks.''

"Yes, it does," he quickly agreed. "In fact, I was
thinking about that.'' He paused, and she had the
sense of him steeling himself. "Best course is for us
to get married, Teri," he stated decisively.

The shock of hearing him suggest what she hadn't
believed was a possibility rocked her for a moment,
letting loose the host of clawing needs that had at-
tacked her in the bedroom.

"But you don't want to get married," she blurted
out before common sense could be eroded by foolish
weakness.

He was visibly discomforted by the reminder.
"This is different," he claimed.

"You're prepared to settle into being a fulltime
husband instead of a sometime lover?'' she shot at
him, unable to believe such a miraculous turnaround.

He couldn't stop a grimace at that prospect. "It'll
take some adjustment," he conceded.

"You don't love me, Leo.''

He frowned, clearly not comfortable with the emotional word. "We get on well, Teri," he argued man-
fully.

"When you're here. Which is not all that frequently. We're hardly talking day-in, day-out stuff, are we?''

"We're both reasonable people. Surely we could respect each other's differences. As we have this past year.''

In limited doses, she thought, only too painfully aware how living together could colour everything differently. "Leo, you're not dying to have me as your wife and you're not my idea of a husband,'' she stated with brutal honesty.

"There is the child to consider, Teri,'' he came back strongly.

"I don't need you to do the honourable thing by me,'' she retorted, hating the idea he was screwing himself up to take her on for the sake of their child.

"It's not honour. Dammit, Teri! I want the child to have my name.''

Male pride! Anger at his one-eyed view spurted off her tongue. "And what's wrong with *my* name? Is Adams too ordinary for your child?''

He rolled his head in exasperation. "It's not that! I just want…'' His eyes blazed with determined possessiveness. "It's my kid, too.''

"I'm not denying it.'' Her own stung pride urged her to add, "But I'm certainly not going to marry you just to give *my* child *your* name.''

His jaw tightened. The strong tension flowing from him suddenly caught at Teri's nerves. This was not sexual tension. This was an entirely different energy force and it was daunting, giving her a jolting insight into the will of the man. Nothing wishy-washy about Leo Kingston. He was very, very different to Wayne.

She watched his eyes sharpen to laser intensity and quivered inside, realising they'd never argued before. This was a side of Leo she had sensed but never seen.

"Do you intend to cut me out, Teri?"

"Out of what?" she asked warily, unsure of her ground with him.

"When you walked away from me downstairs, I had the impression you were more than prepared to shovel me out of your life and the life of our child."

She shook her head at his interpretation of her actions which had been meant to free him of all responsibility. "I left it up to you. The choice was yours," she insisted.

"Then I'm in," he stated firmly.

"If you want to be."

The nerve-jangling tension eased. "I do. Very much," he said emphatically.

It surprised her. Though it shouldn't, she quickly reasoned, given his unexpected proposal of marriage. Yet this strong paternal streak didn't fit into his free-wheeling lifestyle at all. Would it waver once the idea of fatherhood was replaced with realities?

"Okay," she agreed. "I have nothing against our child knowing its father, but I won't marry you, Leo."

He looked relieved, then curious. "Marriage to me could be a good deal for you, you know."

"Only if we spent the rest of our lives in bed," she returned flippantly, offended he should think she'd be persuaded by status considerations. Belatedly remembering the glass in her hand, she lifted it with mocking intent. "I need more than champagne in a husband."

He laughed, his face lighting up with a dancing appreciation she didn't quite comprehend. But she felt his pleasure in her, a wave of warmth that muddled up all her straight thinking...Leo, the lover, eyes flirting wickedly with hers. Even now, when they were seriously discussing the future, he could set her heart pumping overtime and arouse little prickles of excitement in anticipation of what he promised.

"Oh, I don't know," he drawled, his mouth moving into a very sensual smile as he clicked his glass with hers. "I've always thought champagne a great starting point for wonderful things."

"Sex," she said flatly, determined on keeping a proper perspective with Leo.

"Uh-huh. We spend a third of our lives in bed," he said, totally unabashed by her attempted put-down. "And you'd have to admit I deliver on all fronts there." He grinned triumphantly. "We now have positive proof of my potency."

More male pride!

Teri eyed him with arch understanding. "So that's why you're suddenly cock-a-hoop about being a father. Now you know those little fellows of yours can make the grade."

She sashayed around him and headed for the table where the candle was now dripping wax onto the icing of the cake. Better that she keep some distance between them until she had Leo sorted out in her mind. He was lethal to any common sense when he turned on his sexual magnetism.

"Don't knock it!" he aimed after her, still with an exultant lilt in his voice. "Between us, I reckon we're going to make a great kid."

Which surely had to mean he liked the idea of her being the mother of his child. Teri felt a warm kick of pleasure, despite her disapproval of his other attitudes. In his heart, Leo did not feel she was wife material or he wouldn't have limited their relationship the way he had. She suspected he didn't see any woman taking up that role in his life again. But he must be seeing her as good mother material.

"Yes, I think we'll make a great kid, too," she agreed, then half turned to cock an eyebrow at him and ask the critical question. "Do you really intend sticking around to find out, Leo?"

"You bet I am," he answered without the slightest hesitation, his whole face lit with excited anticipation. He strode towards her, arms out expansively, the glass of champagne in his hand in danger of sloshing out its contents. "Any help you want, just ask me, Teri. You won't be on your own with our child. We'll be partners in parenthood. Okay?"

It was a far more generous stance than Teri could have imagined coming from him. She was stunned by it. Partners in parenthood encompassed a lifetime connection. Did he realise that? Had he given it serious consideration or was he riding on some wave of euphoria, revelling in the idea of having a child without really seeing the responsibilities that went with it?

He set his glass down on the tray and blew out the candle. Teri watched the smoke from it wisping upwards, curling, disintegrating, and wondered if Leo's

interest in their child would be like that—a brightly
lit candle tonight, insubstantial smoke in the future.

Then it seemed in one smooth fluid movement he
was behind her, sliding his arms around her waist,
snuggling her body back against his, hotly reminding
her of what they'd shared most in coming to this critical night.

She closed her eyes, savouring the feel of him, the
powerful masculinity that stirred such a deep uncon-
trollable response, like a fountain of sensation bursting into life, arrows of desire shooting through her,
every nerve bridling with delight, skin tingling with
excitement, and spasms of pleasurable anticipation
pulsing inside her.

She'd wanted this contact with him from the moment he'd come striding into the restaurant tonight,
wanted to forget the baby and simply luxuriate in
what Leo could do to her. At least now she could let
it happen. He still wanted her...even with child.

He planted a soft, sensual kiss on the curve of her
neck and shoulder, and she instinctively stretched her
head back to give him more access, loving the way
he tasted her, slowly, seductively, spreading more and
more delicious heat from his mouth. He trailed sweet,
tantalising kisses up to her ear and gently, erotically
teased her lobe with his teeth.

"I'm so hungry for you," he murmured.

"Mmmh..." she blissfully agreed, feeling like a
cat who wanted her coat stroked as she rubbed her
bottom across his thighs. He'd been away three
weeks. She'd missed him. She needed more of him,
more than he was ever likely to give. But her fuzzy

mind quickly shied away from letting that thought break her concentration on the sheer physical thrill of having Leo holding her, kissing her, touching.

His hands slid up to cup her breasts. He squeezed lightly, a kind of gloating possessiveness she normally enjoyed, but a new tenderness there caused her to wince and she lifted her free hand to pluck at his in protest. "Softer," she instructed.

"I hurt you?" He sounded puzzled.

"They're tight, sensitive. The pregnancy, I guess."

"Making changes so soon?"

She sighed. "Must be. They've never felt like this before."

He released them, gliding his hands down to her stomach and lightly pressing in to the flatness there, making her acutely conscious of his state of arousal. "You feel the same to me," he said with satisfaction.

And would for a while, Teri thought, but what then? She was suddenly stricken by doubts again. Leo was hungry for her. Had he put on a paternal act just so he could pleasure himself with her? Torn between the desire to simply give in to his pleasuring and the need for honesty between them, Teri finally blurted out, "I'll probably have a thick waist by the time you drop in again."

"Will that worry you?" he asked, kissing her other shoulder while the caress on her stomach moved lower, causing an almost paralysing rise in sweet tension.

"You might find me less...less desirable," she babbled.

"What? With my son in there?" He gave a low, mellow laugh. "Making love will be twice as good."

His son?

Teri's mind made an abrupt leap into overdrive and a progression of fast and furious activity through her brain waves suppressed the palpitating buzz of sexual promise.

First his drive to give their child *his* name.

Then his pride in his potency.

Now their child had to be a boy.

And he was hungry for sex with her.

This was all macho male testosterone gone mad!

She jerked herself out of his embrace, slapped the glass of champagne she was still holding down on the tray, and swung around in fierce defence of her own gender.

"It might be a girl, Leo."

He looked startled. "A girl?"

"Yes! A girl like me. Not a boy like you. How do you feel about that?"

It was a challenge that was suddenly, vitally important to Teri. Somehow it involved all the shortcomings in their relationship that she tried to keep buried for the sake of having Leo in her life. If they had a daughter, would he care about knowing *her* birthday? Would he care about all the things that made up her day-to-day existence?

He was frowning heavily. "A girl..."

"People do have daughters as well as sons," she reminded him, her voice sharpening as a welling tide of hidden resentments started pushing forward.

He shook his head, still frowning. "I hadn't

thought of a girl. There aren't any girls in my family." He was clearly fumbling with this new view of her pregnancy.

"It's a fifty-fifty chance, Leo," Teri drilled. "You can't count on a son."

"Right," he said, but it was a very weak "right' this time, a token "right' that had no enthusiasm behind it.

The door buzzer for the restaurant sounded, startling both of them. Teri checked her watch—10:26—well past the closing time printed on the front door.

"Did you leave the lights on?" she asked tersely. For her, the celebration had turned sour. The sex had turned sour. Everything had turned sour.

Leo looked befuddled, trying to think. "Yes. I forgot about them."

She gave vent to an exasperated sigh and marched off to the staircase as the buzzer sounded again. In fact, she was glad of the interruption. She hated Leo for being so self-centred, hated herself for wanting a man who was never going to give her the kind of relationship that stood firm in all circumstances. She'd shortchanged herself, but no way was she going to let him shortchange their daughter, just because she wasn't a son.

"I'll come with you," Leo called, hastily striding after her.

"Fine!" she snapped, charging down the hall ahead of him. "And you can keep right on going, too."

"What?"

"You heard me." On down the staircase she went,

seething with the conclusions she'd come to. "I might be twice as good to you if I'm having a son, but I'm obviously only half as good if I have a daughter. If you think I'm going to bed with a man who has such a sexist attitude..."

"I didn't say that!" he protested, making the stairs creak loudly under his heavy feet.

"I should have known," she muttered, furious with her own weakness. "You only ever wanted me for sex. Blowing in when you felt the need for it, then farewell till the next time."

"Now hang on a minute," he argued as she swept through the kitchen. "Don't tell me we haven't had a mutual thing going between us."

"You set the limits to it. Food and sex. Satisfying your appetites." She shot straight into the dining room which was starkly empty of life now, and she emptied out the rest of her rage as she headed for the front door. "You didn't want to spend more time with me beyond that, Leo, and the thought of spending time with a daughter doesn't appeal, does it?"

"I don't know much about little girls. What they want and..."

"Not much about big girls, either," she fired at him.

"For God's sake, Teri! We've enjoyed a lot of times together."

"Food and sex," she repeated relentlessly.

"We talked, too. I like your company, damn it!"

"Not...enough!"

Having reached the door and uncaring of the shadowy figure on the other side of it, she deactivated the lock, and opened up.

"Wait!" Leo commanded, shoving past her to stand guard against any trouble with the person hovering outside. "The restaurant is closed," he stated, his tone terse and uncompromising.

"I know," came the mild reply, the male voice tantalisingly familiar to Teri. "I was hoping... Teri, is that you?"

Recognition burst through her brain and off her lips. "Wayne?"

He laughed at her surprise. "Yeah, it's me. Back home again. Thought I'd drop by and wish you a happy birthday. I brought you a box of your favourite Belgian chocolates."

Another one of his guilt visits!

"Who is this guy, Teri?" Leo demanded bruskly, measuring Wayne as though he were sizing him up for a fight. In actual fact, their height and build were similar, but Wayne's easy-going nature was no match for Leo's powerhouse of energy.

"If I'm intruding..." Wayne gestured his willingness to be off, probably intimidated by the waves of aggression coming at him.

"No," Teri hastened to assure him, realising this particular guilt visit was very timely. "Leo was just leaving, weren't you, Leo?"

Blazing blue eyes sliced to her. "Just who is this guy? And what's he doing, calling on you at this time of night?"

"He's a friend, Leo, an old friend. Some women do have male friends, you know. They even find out things about them, like their birthdays and what their favourite chocolates are.''

His mouth thinned. The acid little criticism was clearly not to his taste. Teri didn't care. Let him burn. He'd had everything his own way for too damned long!

''Yeah, you don't have to worry about me,'' Wayne chimed in cheerfully, intent on lowering the tension. ''Teri and I have known each other since we were kids.''

''Odd she's never mentioned you to me,'' came the bitingly suspicious remark.

He was like a dog protecting his territory, Teri thought, and he had absolutely no right to be possessive. ''Well, Leo, you've never spoken to me about your ex-wife,'' she pointedly reminded him, ''and you've never asked me about my ex-husband.''

He stared at her incredulously. ''Your ex?''

''Husband, yes. Do come in, Wayne.'' She stepped back from the doorway, making room for him to enter, then wriggled her fingers in a miniwave to her erstwhile lover. ''Good night, Leo.''

As she took in his glowering frustration, one part of Teri's mind warned she was probably going to regret giving Leo his marching orders, but the rest of it revelled in savage satisfaction.

However, Wayne didn't quite get past Leo. A hand clamped on his shoulder, halting him in midstride. Wayne jerked his head to Leo, alarm all over his face. He was subjected to a cutting blast from twin blue lasers.

''Just don't start getting any ideas about linking up

with Teri again, Wayne,'' came the blistering command. ''You might be her ex-husband but I'm the father of her child.'' The laser beams were transferred to Teri. ''And I intend *to be* the father of her child. No one's going to cheat me out of my own kid.''

Having delivered this fierce declaration, Leo released Wayne and walked off into the night, satisfied he'd torpedoed any reunion which could threaten his position.

CHAPTER EIGHT

HAVING spent most of the day, trying to focus his distracted mind on nailing all the paperwork on the New Zealand deal, Leo was finally able to pass over the tidy-up details to his ever-efficient assistant. With his office desk mercifully cleared, he relaxed back in his chair, and gave himself up to the same brooding that had consumed his weekend and looked like consuming his entire life.

Who could understand women?

The guy who wrote *Men Are From Mars, Women Are From Venus,* didn't get it right. He should have placed women from Pluto, a dark underworld planet. Venus was purely veneer, the trap to pull men in.

No doubt about that in Leo's mind. Women could be as sweet as honey when they were getting what they wanted, then turn on you like vultures intent on pecking out all your vital parts when you failed to play their game. And you weren't even told the rules!

"Leo?"

"What?" He glared at Mavis for cutting into his finely tuned train of killer thoughts.

She raised her eyebrows at him, disdaining to notice his temperamental mood. "Is there anything else you want filed on the New Zealand trip?"

He had to concede that Mavis Crosby was not from Pluto. Not from Venus, either. She was a nice, homely, middle-aged mother who belonged fairly and squarely on Earth. Neat brown-grey hair, bright brown eyes, green suit, well-cushioned figure, pleasantly lived-in face...very earthy, Mavis was.

Leo always felt comfortable with her. He could trust her to do the right thing all the time. She was reliable, predictable, sensible, the perfect assistant for his business life. Maybe women became normal people after they'd turned fifty.

"I need your advice, Mavis," he said, impulsively deciding to consult her on matters that could not be as foreign to her as they were to him. He waved her to the chair on the other side of his desk. "Stop hovering at that filing cabinet and sit down."

"Ah!" she said with knowing satisfaction, and wasted no time in settling herself to receive his confidence.

Leo grimaced, aware he'd been acting like a bear with a sore head all day. Not even work nor the sense of achievement he should have felt over the New Zealand deal had driven Teri from the forefront of his mind. Teri...having *his* kid, and showing him the door, preferring the company of her *ex-husband.* It burned him every time he thought about it.

"You're a woman, Mavis," he started, inadvertantly glowering at her.

"You can safely say that, yes," she returned dryly.

Not the brightest of starts, Leo thought, and leaned forward, resting his elbows on the desk to fix earnest eye contact. "Now I ask you..." he appealed man-to-man, ignoring the fact he'd established that Mavis was a woman. "For a guy like me...brought up mostly by my Dad because my mother died when I was eight...then sent to an all male boarding school when I was twelve...is it unreasonable for me to be thinking of my still-to-be-born child as a boy?"

Mavis cocked her head, giving him her serious consideration. "Is this a theoretical question, Leo...or is someone expecting your child?"

Good old Mavis...straight to the point. No shilly-shallying around.

"Yes, she is," he affirmed. "Told me on Friday night." He sat back and spread his hands, indicating his own open-mindedness about it all as he explained further. "And there I was, offering her everything a parenting partner should, and what happens?" He rolled his eyes at the sheer irrationality of Teri's behaviour. "She goes off her brain because I didn't think of a girl."

"Ah!" It was the sound of slow and careful digestion of the facts.

Leo waited for some pearls of wisdom. When none was forthcoming, he grew impatient. "Well?" he demanded.

Mavis roused herself out of deep thought. "Are you thinking of marrying this woman, Leo?" she inquired, still not answering his initial question.

He waved a sharp dismissal. "She doesn't want to marry me."

"Ah!" It was a longer *ah* this time, somehow gathering overtones and undertones that suggested Mavis was deeming it wiser to keep her mouth shut in this delicate area.

Which didn't serve Leo's purpose at all. He leaned

forward again, tapping his index finger on the desk to get her mind focused on the critical points.

"It's my kid, Mavis, and she has no right to shoot me out of her life. It's not as if this pregnancy resulted from some one-night stand. We've had a relationship for about a year and never an argument between us until this happened."

He rocked back and threw up his hands as frustration overtook him again. "Suddenly I'm not good enough for her. Not good enough for anything!"

"Uh-huh." Mavis nodded a few times, her shrewd eyes undoubtedly picking up all the body language signals being emitted. Cautiously she inquired, "Am I to understand you want the child, Leo, regardless of whether it's a boy or a girl?"

"Yes, I do," he declared emphatically. "I'm not some fly-by-night sort of guy. You know I've never shirked responsibilities, Mavis. Boy or girl, it's mine."

She nodded again, obviously agreeing with him since she had no reason not to agree. She'd been working with him long enough to know his character inside out. He could count on Mavis to understand what he was telling her.

"And you want my advice," she said, mulling over the situation.

"If you can throw some light..." He shook his head in vexed bewilderment. "It's beyond my understanding. She turned on me as though she'd never once been happy with me. And that's not true, Mavis. I swear it!"

"Pregnancy does make changes, Leo," Mavis advised slowly. "For a woman, nothing is the same as before. You should read up on it. Learn what you're dealing with."

He frowned. Teri had looked the same, felt the same. Nevertheless, Mavis might have a valid point here. Teri certainly hadn't behaved the same.

"I'll get some books," he said, relieved to have an answer he could grasp.

"They might be a bit on the technical side, Leo," Mavis warned. "Try women's magazines. They cover both the physical and the emotional side of pregnancy. There are lots of magazines about having babies available now."

"Right! Good thinking, Mavis. Anything else that might help?"

She hesitated, took a deep breath, eyed him warily, then offered, "Woo the woman."

"Woo? What do you mean...*woo?*"

Mavis sighed as though he were a hopeless case. "I mean give her things to show you care, to show you're thinking of her. Go out of your way to do what she wants. Find out what her needs are..."

The gentle flow of advice hit all the wrong places. "Are you telling me I'm not good enough for any woman unless I play that game?" He slammed his hands on the desk and rose to his feet in towering fury. "What about *my* needs? Is it always a one-way bloody street with women?"

He was too pumped up to wait for a reply. He stormed around his office, all the deeply held resentments from his marriage boiling over into a torrent of explosive energy.

"It's blackmail. A mean, malicious, power game. Grovel at my feet or you won't get what you want from me. Fall into line. Perform, or else. An endless testing of how much you'll do for them. And you're garbage if you don't deliver!"

He smashed a fist down on the desk. "What happened to simply liking each other? Respecting each other's differences? Can't a woman meet a man on mutual ground?"

"Leo, I don't know this woman," Mavis said quietly. "I was only suggesting..."

"It stinks, Mavis! It's the ultimate power grab. To hold a man's child over his head, to beat him into some kind of submission to her will..."

"I didn't say she was doing that, Leo."

"It adds up. It all adds up. Thank you, Mavis. You have made everything abundantly clear to me."

She stood up, taking his words as a dismissal. "Well, Leo, it's your life. Your decision," she granted graciously. "But I'd read up on pregnancy if I were you. That answers a lot, as well. And at the end of the day, there's still the child to be considered."

And giving him one of her wise looks, she sailed out of his office, leaving him to get his feet down to earth again.

CHAPTER NINE

ANOTHER weekend gone, five of them now, Teri despondently acknowledged as she ushered out the last Sunday brunch customer and put the Closed sign on the door. Leo was not coming back. It was stupid to keep fraying her nerves, checking who was entering the restaurant every time the door opened. It was never Leo. She might as well put a Closed sign on everything to do with him, too.

Outside it was fine and warm and sunny. Summer had lingered on into March and daylight saving gave her a long afternoon. She was free now until Tuesday, when another busy week would start, and brooding over the rights and wrongs of her hot-headed decision to cast Leo Kingston out of her future, and the future of their child, was not going to change anything. She had to get on with her life.

Since the weather was pleasant, Teri decided to spend an hour or two in her small backyard, potting her new plants. After all, she couldn't rely on feeling well tomorrow morning. Whoever said pregnancy was a happy state needed their thinking rearranged.

She finished locking up. Leaving Dylan in the kitchen, making up some special dish he wanted to take home to his mother, she headed upstairs to change out of her uniform, donning a pair of old stretch jeans and a comfortable baggy shirt. Her waist had thickened a bit. Not much. But enough for her to be relieved to get out of her snug skirt. She would have to design herself something looser to wear in the restaurant soon.

Her mind inexorably clicked back onto the night of the showdown with Leo. "What child?" Wayne had asked. "No one told me you'd had a child, Teri."

"That's because I haven't," she'd answered.

"Then what was that guy on about?"

She'd spilled it all out, needing a sympathetic ear and a shoulder to cry on, and Wayne, typically, had said not to worry. A guy who was set on killing a rival would definitely be back to fight another day.

Time had proven him wrong about that. Losing might not be in Leo Kingston's normal lexicon, but if winning meant putting up with a woman who dared to criticise his attitudes and who might deliver a daughter instead of a son, winning was clearly not such a great option.

As she sat on the bed to remove her loafers and strap on sandals, Teri told herself for the umpteenth time she was better off without Leo messing her around. She didn't have to worry about his reactions or any interference with her plans for their child. She could suit herself, what she did and how she did it. Being the sole decision-maker was definitely better. Definitely.

Feeling lonely would pass.

She took a deep breath, stood up straight, and with her mind determinedly set on living each day as it came—without Leo—she headed downstairs to get on with what she'd planned. An ironic smile came as she remembered a sign she'd read at some plant nursery—*When society wearies, there is always the garden.* Not that she had a real garden since her backyard was almost completely paved, but pot-plants served the same purpose.

She'd managed to buy a whole stack of small green pots with accompanying saucers very cheaply. By planting clumps of pansies and violas and polyanthus in them, Teri figured she could grow pretty little centrepieces for the tables in the restaurant. It was simply a matter of transferring the seedlings she'd chosen to the pots, and nurturing them along until they bloomed.

The balmy afternoon sunshine and the pleasant prospect of growing flowers lifted her spirits. It didn't take long to get everything she needed out of the storage shed and set it all on the trestle table in the open yard. She was happily scooping the potting mixture out of its bag and into the pots when a sharp, peremptory voice startled her out of her rhythm.

"What the hell do you think you're doing?"

The special mixture of soil and fertilisers in the gardening trowl went flying as she jerked around to find the man who was supposed to be out of her life, striding straight back into it, his face thunderously disapproving and his arms flailing around in vehement protest.

"Pregnant women can get bronchial infections from that stuff," he raved on. "Haven't you read up on things you should avoid?"

Before Teri could catch her breath or put two thoughts together, the trowel was whipped out of her hand and Leo was hauling her away from the trestle table, up to the end of the yard where she'd set a bench seat under the one tree she had. He sat her down and stepped back, obviously winding up to deliver a lecture.

Then he noticed he still had the offending trowel in his hand and tossed it back towards her work station. It knocked some of the pots off the trestle table, fortunately not the ones she'd already filled, but the sheer carelessness of the action snapped Teri out of shock and into fighting mode.

"Just who do you think you are, barging in on me and pushing me around?" she flung at him, her heart thumping, her stomach churning, her mind screaming that he had no right to appear at all after not appearing for so long.

"I thought you were sensible enough to take proper care, Teri," he shot at her, ignoring her question. "I come by to check on you and what do I find?"

"You find me minding my own business," she sliced in, incensed further at his thinking he had the right *to check on her*.

"And taking a stupid risk with your health," he declared with vehement conviction. "There's all sorts of unfriendly chemicals in fertilisers."

She was tempted to say they weren't unfriendly to flowers but in the face of Leo's fierce insistence they were harmful to her in her pregnant state, she wilted into muttering, "I just wanted to pot some plants."

Recognising it was a partial surrender to his will, Leo dropped his belligerent stance, glanced over his shoulder at the trestle table, heaved a sigh, then rolled his gaze back to her. "Tell me what you want done and I'll do it," he stated, determined purpose stamped on his face.

"You?" Incredulity billowed through her mind. "Have you ever potted a plant in your life, Leo?"

His eyes flared icy fire. "Do you get a kick out of cutting me down, Teri?"

She shrivelled inside. Guilt and shame mixed a brew of heat that burned up her neck and scorched her cheeks. Her lashes fluttered down, veiling the uncomfortable twinges of conscience that had plagued her this past month. She certainly hadn't been caring or courteous, not fair, either, the night she'd shut the door on him.

"I was surprised. That's all," she excused limply. "It's not the sort of work I associate with you."

"I don't imagine the task requires skilled labour and I am capable of following instructions," came the biting reply.

Teri took a deep breath and forced her gaze up again. "It's kind of you to offer."

His eyes locked onto hers in a fierce, tense challenge, and it didn't take any intuition to know she had wounded this man's pride very deeply. She had cut him down in front of her ex-husband, criticising him on the limits of their affair when she had happily complied with those limits all along. Her scathing indictment of him had not been deserved.

"It won't be good for the baby if you get an infection," he said tersely, dismissing any notion of kindness.

The baby...he was ramming it down her throat that

he did care about their child. She'd judged him meanly over that, too.

Taking it for granted she would stay where he'd parked her, out of the danger zone, he strode back towards the trestle table, bending to scoop up the spilled pots as he went. He examined those she'd already filled and remarked, "I take it these contain the correct amount?"

"Yes. The mixture needs packing down a bit but that's the level I want," she answered matter-of-factly, trying to take her cue from him and silently resolving not to say anything contentious.

Dylan must have let him in, she reasoned. A nice surprise and one she'd welcome, her chef had undoubtedly thought, not knowing of the ruction between them. And seeing him again, Teri had to admit it *was* a welcome surprise.

Whatever it meant, she was glad he was here. Maybe something reasonable could be sorted out between them. In her heart of hearts, she had wished for another chance to discuss some possible future between them. After all, he was the father of her child. Not to mention the best lover she could ever imagine having.

He looked great—the black jeans and red cotton knit shirt clinging to his powerful physique. She found her own muscles clenching in need and yearning for the intimacy she had thrown away. Attraction had nothing to do with common sense, she reflected. It was so strong right now, it was difficult to cling to any rational thought at all.

She watched him dipping the trowel into the bag

of potting mixture and measuring out how much gave the right result. A natural bent for efficiency, she thought. No messing around. Get the job done. There was not the pleasure in it that she would have taken. Another difference between them.

So what? she argued. He was doing it for her and it didn't relate to either food or sex. Or maybe he was doing it for the baby, keeping *his* child safe. Either way, she couldn't call it a self-centred action. Hope for better things arising from this visit took a mega-leap.

It was a very real pleasure just to see him again. The afternoon sunshine gleamed on his hair, lustrous black waves, less tamed than usual and actually kicking into curls around the back of his shirt collar. He'd never worn it so long before. She wondered if he hadn't found the time to get it cut, or whether he couldn't be bothered. Her own hair needed a trim. She hadn't felt in the mood to visit her chatter-box hairdresser, but she must do it soon.

"How do you want these plants distributed?" Leo asked, frowning at the labels on the punnets of seedlings.

"Each polyanthus gets a pot of its own," she answered, eagerness creeping into her voice. It was really nice of him to help. "I thought I'd do three pansies and three violas in the others."

"All the same colour in the one pot?"

"No. A mix. The pansy seedlings are mixed already so you don't have to worry about choosing. With the violas, I planned to put one yellow, one apricot and one white in each pot."

"Right!"

"Leave a bit of space between them so the roots can spread out," she added anxiously.

He slanted her a sardonic look. "I may not be a gardener, but I'm not short on logic, Teri."

"Sorry. You did ask for instructions."

He worked on, without acknowledging her remark.

Teri sighed, wishing he wasn't thinking badly of her. They *had* enjoyed a lot of good times together. Her gaze followed the deft movements of his hands...hands that knew how to caress and excite and...she missed their touch, the comfort and pleasure they gave.

Had he missed her? Was that why he'd come, or was it simply to check on her...the mother of a child that might be the son he fancied...a boy in his own image?

Teri caught herself back from pursuing that grudge against him. She didn't know what was in Leo's mind. It was wrong to leap to possibly false assumptions. Sooner or later he would tell her what he wanted and then she would deal with it, maintaining due courtesy instead of reacting impetuously and meanly.

After all, he might have decided having a daughter wasn't so bad. She hadn't given him time to think about it when he'd fumbled the question, going off like a rocket and exploding into a destructive tirade.

Maybe she'd been suffering some hormonal imbalance from being pregnant. She certainly hadn't been well balanced at all. In fact, underneath her supposedly sensible reasoning that day, she'd been riding an emotional roller-coaster from the moment the doctor had given her the test results.

"How have you been, Teri?"

She jerked her gaze up from his hands, but if he had been looking at her, she'd missed it. "Oh, not too bad," she answered airily, determined on not being negative about anything.

He shot her a beetling frown. "No nausea?"

"Well, yes. A bit. Mostly in the mornings."

"Just whoozy or are you throwing up?"

She made an ironic grimace. "The whooziness tends to lead to throwing up."

"Are you doing anything about it?"

"I'm not taking drugs, if that's what you're asking." After his blast on chemicals, Teri figured it was his main concern. "I'm not entirely stupid, Leo," she added dryly. "I just hadn't heard anything bad about potting mixture."

"Heard?" Another beetling frown. "Haven't you been reading up on what you should and shouldn't be doing?"

Teri bit her lips and studied the dappled shade of the tree on the paving stones. The truth was she'd felt too down to read up on pregnancy. The truth was she'd been doing her best to ignore it as far as possible. It was easier not to make a big thing of it when there was no one to share it with.

The only person she'd told, apart from Leo, was Wayne, and she'd sworn him to secrecy. She saw no point in upsetting her family until she had to. They weren't going to like her being a single mother.

"Teri? Is something wrong?"

The anxious concern in his voice had to be answered. She looked up with a wry smile and a little shrug. "I thought having a baby was a fairly natural thing, Leo. It is what women are made for. I figured if I just took it as it came…"

"Don't you care about our child?"

Care? Now that was one step too far. *He* wasn't being fair to suggest any such thing. "Of course, I do," she retorted emphatically, her temperature rising at the implied criticism. "But I don't have time to obsess about it," she went on, heating up as she listed what she had to cope with. "I'm up early to go to the markets and I'm fighting morning sickness the whole time I'm buying food. Then it's back here to prepare lunch. By the time that crowd's gone, I'm so tired I have to take a nap before the evening rush starts. After I close up at night, I fall into bed."

She paused for breath, glaring belligerently at him. There he was, glowing with health and vitality, nothing different about *his* body, no side effects from having done the job of fertilising *her*. She was the one left carrying the baby and now he had the hide to suggest she wasn't doing it right.

"So, Mr. Know-it-all," she fired at him. "When do you suggest I read up on all the possible risk factors pertaining to my condition? I suppose you're going to say I should be doing it now instead of taking a break outside on a sunny afternoon, doing something I enjoy?"

"No," he said quietly. "It's perfectly reasonable you should need and want a break."

She should have been mollified. Yet somehow, seeing him looking so coolly in control struck her as even more unfair. "Well, thank you," she snapped. "If you were nine weeks pregnant with our child, you might not feel quite so efficient and on the ball yourself."

His face tightened. His mouth thinned. His eyes glittered so fiercely it hurt to look at him.

Teri closed her eyes and felt her heart sinking. She'd done it again. Despite all her good resolutions, she'd used Leo as a whipping boy because she'd had a miserable time by herself. He'd only been expressing concern for their child. How was he supposed to know she'd been aching for comfort and reassurance and help, wishing she hadn't sent him away, remembering how he'd promised whatever support she needed?

There was no satisfaction or pride in being independent when she was struggling with the downside of being pregnant. Though, to be absolutely honest, she really wanted someone to care about her, not the baby. She could hardly expect that from Leo after she'd flung a preference for her ex-husband in his face.

She heard water splashing and realised he'd turned on the outside tap. Washing his hands, cleaning off the dirt, getting ready to go, no doubt. No pleasure in staying with a shrewish woman who had nothing good to say to you.

Wearily, despondently, Teri opened her eyes to watch him leave. He turned off the tap and wiped his hands on the raggy old towel that hung from a nail on the wall of the shed. She didn't look at his face, didn't want to see the cold rejection there.

"Thank you for potting the plants for me, Leo," she said, aware her appreciation of his generosity was too little and too late.

"I'm not finished."

"I'm sure what you've done will be enough," she assured him, having lost interest in the project. She was never going to enjoy the pot plants now. Every bit of growth they had would be a reminder of having stunted any possible growth to a relationship with Leo.

"I meant I'm not finished with you, Teri, and I will not be dismissed this time."

The hard, purposeful words thumped into her heart, reviving hope. Her mind zinged with the heady anticipation of getting another chance. Or did he mean— her stomach cramped—he had some cutting down to do himself before walking out on her?

He covered the ground between them like a warrior pumped up to meet and demolish an enemy, striding with that arrogant carriage he had, emanating a total confidence in taking all before him. Teri was suddenly paralysed with confusion. All she could do was stare at him coming at her and wait for the hit.

"Now get this, Teri, and get it good!" he fired at point-blank range, his eyes blazing into hers, intent on burning off any opposition.

He grabbed her upper arms and lifted her up for a direct and close face-to-face confrontation, no quarter given. The full force of his energy hit her with mesmerising impact. When he started telling her what she had to get, she felt like a limp sponge being filled by a fire-hose on full power.

"*You* are going to marry me. *You* are going to do this because it's the *right* thing to do. It takes *two* people to make a child. It takes *two* people to do right by their child. And *we* are going to do that together, whether you like it or not. Have you got that?"

CHAPTER TEN

LEO WANTED to marry her?

Insisting that she marry him?

Despite all she'd said and done?

Teri's mouth fell open in sheer shock.

No words came. Her mind was thrown into utter chaos, all her previous thoughts smashed by this incredible stance from a man who…whose mouth was crashing onto hers.

There was no seductive pleading or persuasion in his kiss. It was hard and hot and urgent, passionately compelling, not seeking her surrender to his will but commanding it. Teri felt bombarded at first, still reeling from the verbal blast. Then the taste of him, the excitement Leo had always stirred, electrified her senses, triggering a greed that surged into a wild and wanton response.

Like a violent rainstorm after a long drought, the need for him beat through her, shooting rivulets of pleasure everywhere, filling the empty spaces that loneliness had dug, making her feel alive and very much a woman again. She moved instinctively, the desire to have his warmth and strength seeping into her so compelling, her arms broke Leo's hold in their eagerness to wind around his neck and pull him closer. Her body virtually sighed with contentment as she nestled it against his, revelling in feeling him as much as she could.

A wild exultation streamed through her as Leo clutched her buttocks, squeezing and lifting, fitting her into the cradle of his loins, letting her know and feel the excitement she aroused in him. Yes, her mind sang, loving the hard evidence of his arousal, anticipating the intimacy that would surely follow, the glorious togetherness they had enjoyed so many times in the past.

His tongue tangled erotically with hers, evoking the mating she yearned for, and she blissfully encouraged him, wanting all he was implicitly promising her. She'd lost track of everything that had parted them before. Only this was real, the sharing of themselves in a sexual heat that pulsed through both of them, building to an exhilarating fusion.

Except Leo didn't pursue it.

With bewildering abruptness, he broke the intimate contact with her, ending their kiss, easing himself back from her, his hands moving to her waist to stop her from closing the space he'd made between them.

Teri's nerves instantly jangled, screaming a silent protest at the loss of singing pleasure. Her mind, still clouded with brilliantly satisfying sensation, was slow to accept the fading of it. She opened her eyes, urgently searching for reason, and found him grim-faced, restraint and determination stamped on every feature.

"Don't you deny that was mutual, Teri, because you're a damned liar if you do," he bit out fiercely, his eyes searing hers with unshakable belief in what she'd just poured out to him.

Her hands had slid to his shoulders as he'd pulled away and she could feel the bunched muscles there, the tension of control mastering desire. He was *not* going to pursue it, regardless of how pumped up his body was with need.

A sense of loss cramped her stomach. Her heart, which had been pounding with wild elation, dropped a beat as it clogged with fear. The realisation sliced through the fog in her mind... Leo had not come to her as the lover he had been. She had wrecked that. Today he was an antagonist, fighting for his rights, seizing on a truth he had unmistakably demonstrated.

Food and sex, she'd thrown at him, as though she'd been insulted by his needs, while the truth was she'd been glad of both of them. And she was glad he was here now, giving her a chance to repair the damage she'd done, to overlay her harsh words with what she really felt about him.

"It was mutual, Leo," she acknowledged quietly.

"It was always mutual," he insisted.

"Yes," she agreed.

"You wanted me as much as I wanted you."

"Yes."

"And you still do."

"Yes."

"So that's something good we've got together if you're honest about it."

She saw the unrelenting challenge in his eyes and sensed a deep hurt and a bitter disillusionment that had been in place long before she'd ever met Leo. In a flash of sharp intuition, she knew her own reckless words had scraped old wounds raw again, and but for their child, he would not have revisited her.

"I'm sorry if I gave you the impression I didn't value what we'd shared," she said, determined now on being honest with him, her eyes eloquently begging his belief. "I did, Leo. Very much. It was just that when I found out about the baby, I guess I wanted...needed...more from you. And I didn't think I'd get it."

Anger kindled in his eyes. He reared back another step, effectively removing all physical contact between them. "I offered you support," he reminded her.

"I know you did. But after the marriage offer...you'd been so adamant against marriage...I knew you couldn't want it...then moving straight onto sex, which was what our affair was all about...the offer of support was...well, it wasn't real to me, Leo."

"I have never lied to you, Teri. Never made false promises. Never tried to mislead you or..."

"Please...I know you haven't. It was just..." She shook her head in anguished self-recrimination. Her hands fluttered in an agitated appeal as she desperately searched for an explanation he might understand. "I was reacting to things," she pleaded. "It was a...a big day for me, Leo. I prepared myself not to expect anything from you and then I felt...out of control. I'm sorry. You threw everything into chaos for me with almost all you said and did."

He frowned. "You didn't think I was a decent enough man to shoulder my responsibilities?"

"Leo, how was I to know? I was scared you'd think I was trying to tie you to me. Having a child isn't a free and easy thing. You'd laid down your terms..."

"I said this was different."

She gathered up one more effort to get through to him, her eyes wearily mocking the hard righteousness in his. "We'd had almost a year of something else. You think that can be turned around in an instant?"

His mouth momentarily tightened. Then slowly he expelled a long, pent-up breath. The anger faded into a neutral expression. "Fair enough. But I meant everything I said, Teri, and it's more than apparent it's no good your being on your own. The most sensible course of action is to let me fix the situation so you can take proper care."

"How do you mean?" she asked warily.

Intense resolution regathered and spoke. "You said you wanted more from me. You've got it. Every bit of support you need. It's obvious you're running yourself ragged and not getting enough rest. You need more staff to help run the restaurant and take the load off you. I'll organise it. Pay for it. Anything you want."

"That's very generous of you, Leo, but the restaurant is mine and..."

"Dammit, Teri! We're in this together. And I don't want you living alone here. Anything could happen to you. You'd better move in with me so I can keep an eye on you while we're waiting to get married."

Married!...there it was again and nothing indecisive about it, either. Teri's heart hopped, skipped and jumped all over the place. He had meant it then...marriage for the sake of their child. And mutual sexual pleasure to help it stick.

Her head went dizzy, thinking about it. She stumbled back and sat down on the bench seat, trying to get her bearings on this extraordinary offer. It wasn't an empty commitment, as she'd thought last time. He was filing his stake in the future of his child. Their child.

"Are you okay?" In an instant Leo was down on his haunches in front of her scanning her face with urgent concern. "You've gone quite pale. Take some deep breaths and move your legs around, Teri."

"What?"

"It gets the blood flowing freely. Fainting is quite common during the first trimester of pregnancy. It's because increased progesterone causes the blood vessels to relax, and it takes longer for oxygen to reach the brain."

She shook her head in dazed bemusement at Leo being a font of information on her state. "I'm not about to faint," she assured him.

"You don't look good," he said worriedly.

The vivid blue eyes were still projecting caring...*caring for her.* Or was that mixed up with her having his child? With him crouched so near, her heart was pumping too madly for her to think straight.

"I just didn't expect you to make another marriage proposal," she blurted out. "I don't know how to take it."

"It's the logical step in the circumstances," he argued.

Logic had very little to do with feelings, Teri thought. "Are you sure you want this, Leo?" she probed.

"Yes. I see no other way to get things right," he said forcefully, eyes ablaze with intensity of purpose. "We've got to make this a real partnership, Teri, and I promise you I'll pull my weight. If you can bring yourself to meet me halfway, I'm sure we can make it work. For all three of us."

On the principle that where there's a will, there's a way, Teri thought, and the feverish hope pounding through her heart lost its wild momentum. A cold practicality swept the dizziness from her mind. She wondered if a rational commitment to a future together was a better basis for marriage than the rosy expectations that bloomed from a love-based relationship.

She had *believed* in a future with Wayne.

Leo was bluntly proposing they work at it.

Trying to see it from his point of view, Teri figured they had three things going for them—undeniably great sex, a similar taste in food, and a child they both wanted the best for.

The last consideration was by far the most important, obviously the driving force behind the proposal, and Teri was strongly swayed by it, though she couldn't help feeling…let down…by the starkness of Leo's logic. Couldn't he *feel* some personal gratification—apart from getting good sex—in having *her* as his wife?

She wanted to be at least special to the man she married. Did being the mother of his child make her special enough to Leo? It felt *second-hand* to Teri, yet regardless of any failings Leo might have, she did want to keep him in her life. She'd never felt so drawn to anyone else, not even Wayne. And the past month had stamped home that being alone and pregnant and thirty years old was not a happy state.

She took a deep breath and said, "Maybe it's worth a try."

"A try?" Leo jerked up to his full height, anger unfurling, as well. "'A try'?" he repeated contemptuously. "What kind of wishy-washy approach is that? I hand you a full-on commitment and you're only prepared to put me on trial?"

Rigid with disgust, he stalked away from her.

Agitated by his negative reaction, Teri stood up to call him back. "You haven't exactly led up to this proposition, Leo. We might not like living together. There are lots of things to consider."

"No, there's not!" He whirled around, jabbing a finger at her. "There's only one consideration, Teri. Our child. And it's time you started thinking about it instead of pretending it doesn't need any of your attention."

The criticism rankled. Her chin shot up and a flush of pride burned into her cheeks. "I have a life, too, Leo."

"So have I," he retorted. "And I hope to God, you'll have the decency to respect it as I'll respect yours, because our lives have merged, Teri, and there's no going back to being selfishly single. Not if you care about the welfare of our child.''

"Fine!" she snapped, the accusation of selfishness hitting directly on her past experience of him having everything *his* way. Which he seemed to be setting up again. "Then how come I have to move in with you?" she shot at him. "Why don't you move in with me?"

He strode back aggressively as he answered, "Because *my* home is not connected to business premises where you're on call day and night. It has three bedrooms, one of which you can turn into a nursery." He stopped a metre away from her and gestured dismissively at the limited space around where they stood. "And the backyard is much bigger than this one, providing a reasonable playing area."

All cogent points, yet Teri couldn't help resenting his high-handed attitude, judging the issue instead of discussing it with her. "I'd want to see your place for myself before I agree to move into it," she argued.

"Then let's go and settle the question now," he retorted, seizing the initiative with glowering contempt for what he undoubtedly saw as petty arguments.

Furious with him for snatching the moral high ground and making her feel mean, she tersely reminded him, "You realise, of course, you've never invited me into your home before."

"With good reason." His eyes flashed hard suspicion. "Just remember I've never criticised how you've got yourself set up here. Everyone's entitled to their own sense of comfort."

Teri folded her arms and glared at him. "So I'm supposed to just fit in with you, am I? Don't touch anything? Don't change anything?" It was the same old scenario with Leo, and she wasn't about to continue it, not into a marriage. She raised her eyebrows in mocking challenge. "Precisely what was it you said about meeting halfway?"

His eyes narrowed on her belligerent stance. "We accommodate each other. Okay?"

"As long as we have that firm understanding," she agreed.

He heaved a deep sigh, expelling the explosive energy and settling himself into calm logic again. His eyes commanded the same from her as he stated, "I'm not an unreasonable man, Teri. I won't disregard your needs. I don't want mine disregarded, either. If that means compromise, I suggest we do it with as good a grace as we can muster."

"Fair enough," she accepted, her own temper cooling as she realised they had moved several steps forward in their involvement with each other.

Her curiosity was deeply piqued by his reservations in letting her into his home. She had the weird impression he was protecting a vulnerability he didn't want to lay open, and she wondered if he ever actually admitted anyone to his private life. He wasn't doing it for her, she realised. Most probably, he would never have done it for her. It was his child who had broken this barrier...a part of himself he couldn't shut out.

"Are you up to walking three blocks?" he asked bruskly. "I'll call a taxi if..."

"No. A walk will do me good."

"As you wish." He waved her forward to join him.

Teri held her ground. "Just one question first, Leo. How keen will you be on this marriage if our child turns out to be a daughter instead of a son?"

"I'll be giving either one a father who cares enough to provide a family unit for them. Can their mother say as much?"

She held his fierce challenge and threw it back at him. "Oh, their mother cares enough not to land her child in a *dysfunctional* family unit. Which is why we test the ground first, Leo."

His jaw tightened. His gaze raked down to her stomach and back again. "Well, you do hold all the cards, don't you, Teri?" he mocked savagely. "As long as I want my child, you can crack the whip and lay down the law because I have no legal rights. It's a nice little power game...holding off on marriage...seeing how far I'll dance to your tune."

It was like a hard, cold slap in the face, both shocking and highly sobering. She hadn't really stopped to think where he was coming from...a single father without any legal rights to his child...fighting for a foothold in a life she could deny him, simply by virtue of the fact she was the one who'd give birth.

"I wouldn't do that to you, Leo," she blurted out, her heart turning over at how blindly self-centred she had been in her arguments.

His eyes bored into hers, ruthlessly intent on probing her motives. "Then what are you doing, Teri? Why do you keep cutting down my plan for the future? Is your plan so much better, keeping our child to yourself?''

She flushed. "I don't know. I just don't see it in the same clear-cut way you do. I'm sorry if that offends you. I'm asking you for time. That's all."

"No. You're asking for more than that. But let me tell you, I'm not elastic you can keep stretching. Every person has a breaking point. You'd better start figuring out what you want because one day you'll have to answer to our child for your decisions."

He stepped aside, pride and dignity underlining his scorn for her equivocations. "Perhaps a walk will do us both good," he said with very dry irony. "Ready?"

"Yes."

She felt so shaken, she had to force her legs forward to fall into step beside him and go where he led. His home would reveal more about him, she thought, grasping at something concrete to hang on to. Leo had shattered her *one day at a time, take it as it comes* plan for dealing with her pregnancy. She couldn't go back to it. Though she couldn't feel comfortable about what he'd draw her into, either.

Would he be a good husband?

A good father?

There were worse things than being a single mother.

She had no real cause not to trust him, Teri reflected, glancing at the plants he'd potted as they passed the trestle table. He'd done that for her because she'd wanted it done. It was a measure of unselfish giving. And she couldn't say he wasn't taking the responsibility of parenthood to heart.

She suspected marriage was the ultimate sacrifice for him, an intrusion on his life he was struggling to tolerate for the sake of having his child. Maybe she should be more prepared to make sacrifices, too. Nothing was achieved without a cost. Certainly the willpower he was pouring into his decision impressed her. Very deeply.

The champagne man was not all fizz.

In fact, compared to Wayne, Leo might very well be a rock of stability. And that was worth having. It was something Teri really wanted in a man, especially in a life partner. It was hard, shouldering all the responsibilities. Another set of shoulders—strong, reliable ones—would make everything much easier. And there was a lot more of Leo she wanted, too, underneath all her fighting words.

She needed to have those critical items firmly imprinted on her mind before she opened her mouth again. Leo's warning felt very ominous. Stretch him too far…and snap! He wasn't made of elastic. No one was. And if inside his current stony exterior beat a good and caring heart, what a fool she'd be to drive him away!

CHAPTER ELEVEN

MARRIAGE!

Leo shook his head, barely able to believe he was fool enough to be fighting for it. Moreover, with a woman who looked like giving him as hard a time as Serena. Though, by God! he wasn't about to be taken for a ride in *this* marriage.

If Teri agreed to it.

Which she ought to, if she had any sense at all.

Having reached the back door to the restaurant kitchen, he paused to let her precede him inside. She flicked a glance at him and her eyes had such a poignant look of vulnerability, he was torn between the urge to wrap her in his arms and promise her she'd be safe in his keeping, and a more savage impulse to shake her into getting her priorities right.

It was perfectly obvious she needed him. But was she fair-minded enough to admit that? No! One look was all it had taken him to know he had to step in and get some appropriate management in place.

Her face was drawn with fatigue, her hair—which she'd always kept stylishly trim—was dull and almost shaggy, and her ignorance about the potting mixture...well, she'd explained that but the explanation itself was a clear manifesto for his intervention.

"Dylan's gone," she commented, frowning at the

clean and deserted kitchen. "He should have checked with me before he left."

"He was tidying up when I arrived. Probably didn't want to butt in to say goodbye," Leo excused.

She nodded, still frowning. "I hope he didn't over-hear..." She sighed. "I guess they have to know I'm pregnant sooner or later."

The sooner, the better, in Leo's opinion. Then, at least, her staff could be watching out for her. He was sure she'd been on the verge of fainting earlier. He'd speak to Dylan himself about that. Speak to Dylan about more staff, too. The young chef might know someone who could fill in for Teri. Personal knowledge was better than advertising for help. In a small business like this, it was important for everyone to get on well with each other.

He watched Teri lift a key ring from a hook above the kitchen counter and proceed to lock the back door. Her baggy shirt somehow emphasised her fragility. She was losing weight instead of putting it on. When he'd held her close he'd felt the difference, though she'd still felt good. More than good.

As she checked that the lock was activated, his gaze dropped to her delectable backside, remember-ing the feel of her soft, sexy cheeks. The long shirt covered them, frustrating any visual pleasure, but he still stirred at the memory of how she'd responded to feeling him. At least his bed in this marriage shouldn't be a bargaining couch. No way would he allow it to become one, either!

"Done!" She swung around, and strode off into the dining room, leaving him to follow.

Leo strolled after her, suddenly reminded of the last time Teri had led him to the front door of the restaurant, shutting him out on the street and letting her ex-husband in. A host of highly basic and primitive instincts stirred.

Precisely *what* was Teri's relationship with her ex-husband?

Wayne she'd called him. Wayne with a box of her favourite Belgian chocolates. *Woo the woman,* Mavis had said. Had Wayne come wooing Teri that night? If so, how far had he got?

Teri was a very sexy woman. What's more, she enjoyed sex. She'd cut him off that night and he'd been in New Zealand for three weeks before that. It was nine weeks in all since they'd last gone to bed together. But surely she wouldn't...not with her *ex.*

She unlocked the front door and held it open for him to go out ahead of her. Leo swiftly noted there was no one lingering on the sidewalk this afternoon. All the same, he didn't move far, making sure Teri stepped out after him.

He watched her lock up again, brooding over the way she had welcomed Wayne. *Old friends.* If they were such good old friends, how come they weren't still married?

Which raised other prickly questions.

The pregnancy had been an accident. Teri wasn't keen on marrying him, despite his being the father of their child. Was she still hankering for her ex, wanting a second chance at marriage with him?

Leo didn't care for that thought at all.

Not one bit.

Having finished locking up, Teri pocketed the key ring and offered him a wry little smile. "So...lead me to your cave, Leo."

"Right!" he growled. "And you can tell me about Wayne on the way!"

CHAPTER TWELVE

TERI was wishing she'd taken the time to change her gardening clothes for something that matched up to Leo's smart casual attire. Having Wayne's name thrown at her wiped out the self-conscious feeling of looking frumpy. Her mind was jolted into a highly embarrassed recollection of shuttling Leo off in favour of her ex-husband's company, right here in this doorway.

"I'm sorry..." The words spilled out before she had time to formulate more.

Leo's eyebrows beetled down. "What for?"

"Using Wayne to...to..."

"To get rid of me?" he finished harshly.

"There's a...a comfort in old familiarity when you're in turmoil, Leo," she hastily explained.

"Uh-huh." His eyes grimly assessed her embarrassment. Then in a dry, sardonic tone, he commented, "I'd find no comfort whatsoever in my ex-wife's company. But perhaps your divorce was more amicable."

"Yes. I mean...I don't know about yours. Wayne and I...it was better for both of us to separate. But we still wish each other well."

"Very civilised."

The remark had a sour note to it that churned up Teri's stomach. She remembered Wayne's opinion that Leo had been lethally jealous. She hadn't believed it at the time, thinking a lacerated ego far more likely, not to mention sexual frustration. Jealousy implied more caring than Leo had ever shown her. Though he had bought her the Escada sunglasses. In fact, he'd always been nice to her, made her feel good about herself for the most part. And today...

"We go this way," he said, a flick of his hand indicating direction as he set off, turning up Elizabeth Street towards Oxford.

There was no taking her arm. No catching her hand. He assumed she'd accompany him since she'd agreed to it and Teri did so, but she was acutely conscious of his choice to walk apart. She would have liked some touching, a semblance of togetherness. The question of how much he cared kept tormenting her.

"Do you want to get back together with Wayne?"

The terse question startled her into glancing sharply at him, but he was looking straight ahead, his expression closed to her. *Was* he jealous?

"No. Not in any intimate sense," she assured him, hoping he wasn't imagining she'd had sex with her ex. "That's just not on, Leo," she stated emphatically.

"But you don't mind him visiting you."

That night was certainly sticking in Leo's craw. In all fairness, Teri couldn't blame him for thinking the worst. Playing one man off against another wasn't smart, and she'd really had no cause to do it to Leo. An explanation was due, particularly in these circumstances.

"Wayne usually drops in on me whenever he comes home from wherever he's been. It amounts to once or twice a year and is more or less a catch-up visit on where we are now. A guilt thing, as well, for walking out on our marriage. He checks to see I'm okay."

"He walked out?"

Leo halted, just as they were about to round the corner into Oxford Street. He turned to her and it was like being hit by a paralysing electric charge. Teri's feet stopped dead. Her heart contracted. She had always been aware of an energy force in Leo, a magnetism she'd been drawn to, despite knowing he wasn't seriously engaged with her.

The voltage was suddenly immeasurably stronger and harder-edged, and she had an instant memory flash of him coming towards her in the backyard, a warrior intent on blasting any opposition, very seriously engaged in achieving his purpose.

"Let me get this straight," he aimed directly at her, his eyes scouring hers for hidden traps. "Wayne walked out on your marriage and you still welcome him with open arms?"

Teri took a deep breath, needing to get some oxygen back in her brain. She tried to review what she'd said and belatedly realised it must have sounded inconsistent to Leo. To his mind, it didn't add up, which meant she was *lying* to him and he didn't like it.

He wanted honesty. He'd demanded it of her over the sexual issue and was pushing for it now over Wayne. It was a case of stand and deliver or else! No equivocation. He might want marriage for the sake of their child but he wasn't about to tolerate any two-timing from her.

Which meant he cared about what kind of relationship they'd have, too. Good sex wasn't enough for him. He wanted more. Respect and trust. Both of which were important to her, as well. Conscious of laying a foundation for their possible future together, Teri decided to hold nothing back, even though it meant revealing failures she preferred to forget.

"Wayne and I go back a long way, Leo. We lived in the same neighbourhood as kids. He was always in and out of our house with my brothers. They were best friends. We grew up together, went out together, eventually had sex together. It was the accepted thing that we'd get married. Which we did. Too young to know any better."

"But you must have known each other well," he said, frowning over the scenario she'd drawn.

"I guess there are always two sides of a coin," she answered ruefully. "Wayne has a winning, easy-going charm. It's almost impossible not to like him. But he's a natural born lily of the field. He believes something will always turn up for him instead of working hard at it."

"That didn't sit well with you?" he asked assessingly.

She shrugged. "I'm a natural born worrier. I try to manage things. Which was impossible with Wayne. Money slid through his fingers. Budgeting was an alien word to him. Trying to get him to take responsibility for anything was...well, it was easier to do it myself."

Leo grunted, his eyes flickering slightly as though he'd been plagued by the same experience. The force-field he'd generated eased and there was a less confrontational, more sympathetic air about him as he asked, "How long did you stay together?"

"Three years." Encouraged by the feeling he was really listening, Teri explained further. "Wayne was a guitarist in a band which he always reckoned would make the big time, given a lucky break, but the break never came and the band gradually drifted apart. I'd worked my way up from waitress to managing the kitchen in the local club and I wanted Wayne to get a regular job and settle down. When I talked about getting some security so we could eventually start a family, I think Wayne saw it as four walls closing in on him."

"So he opted for freedom."

"Yes. Basically, we wanted different things out of life. It hurt at the time. I'd invested so much of myself in trying to make things work between us, and then I had to face up to the fact it was hurting both of us, turning me into a nag filled up with frustration, making Wayne feel pressured beyond his capacity to deliver what I wanted of him."

Leo nodded, understanding evident in the softening of his eyes.

Teri flashed him a wry smile. "Which hardly recommends me as a wife, does it?"

His mouth twitched. "Pressure I can handle and security I can deliver. Which makes me an eminently suitable husband for you, wouldn't you say?"

Having neatly sidelined those possible arguments

against their marriage and jettisoned his suspicions about Wayne, Leo exuded the confidence of a conqueror as he tucked her arm around his and proceeded to escort her down Oxford Street.

The man in possession, Teri thought giddily, swamped by the sense that Leo Kingston was not to be shaken from any purpose he set his mind on. It was not surprising he had built himself a successful business. She had been wrong to name him the champagne man, though he could still inject an exciting fizz in her blood.

A lovely warm haze spread through her mind, seductively whispering she could lean on him, be carried along by him, and she'd be safe because he could be counted upon to support her and their child. He was strong and determined and he knew where he was going. Not like Wayne. Not like Wayne at all.

Ahead of them customers of the Kitty O'Shea Hotel had spilled out onto the pavement and it was evident from their raucous voices and unsteady behaviour they'd probably been drinking for hours. It was a popular pub on Sunday afternoons, featuring a live band playing Irish songs, and while the mood of these beer-swilling patrons was definitely merry, not aggressive, Leo smoothly changed position, sliding behind her to take her other arm and place himself between her and any unwelcome attention.

Nothing was said. Nothing untoward happened as they passed by. Yet Teri was intensely conscious of the protection Leo had instinctively given her. Once they were clear of the rowdy mob, he moved back to take the side closer to the street traffic again. It was nice to be looked after, Teri thought, and pride in her independence took another tumble.

Maybe it was general fatigue, or the extra responsibility of her pregnancy, or the loneliness of always having to look out for herself, but the appeal of having a strong capable man at her side struck deep. It wasn't until he led her into Jersey Road that it occurred to Teri she should question Leo about his marriage. Why hadn't *it* been given the full-on commitment he was promising her?

"What happened to your first marriage?" she bluntly asked, glancing at his face to watch his response.

There was a slight tightening of his jaw, a flash of derision from his eyes. "Your rolling stone ex-husband wasn't keen on gathering moss but my ex-wife was intent on gathering all the moss she could get before letting me know she had no intention of honouring her promises."

The acid comment clearly rose from a deep residue of bitterness. No one liked being used, Teri thought, or abused. She began to get a glimmering of why Leo had kept his distance, limiting their relationship to brief bouts of mutual enjoyment where nothing really was asked of either of them. No promises given. None to be honoured or not honoured. Which was precisely why his proposal of marriage had come as such a shock to her.

"Why did you marry her?" she asked.

"Oh, I was totally infatuated at the time," he answered self-mockingly. "And flattered, I suppose."

"Flattered?" Teri queried.

"Serena exuded class and style and winning her seemed like part of the success package. Which she pushed relentlessly after we were married. The right clothes, the right jewellery, the right house, the right vacations, the right social circle…''

The cynicism in his voice eased the little stab of inferiority Teri felt at his first words. The "right' image had clearly lost any importance to Leo though the *Escada* sunglasses undoubtedly reflected his *training* in designer wear by the svelte and sophisticated Serena. Nevertheless, Teri couldn't help wondering if Leo's dalliance with herself was a backlash, considering she worked in the service industry and couldn't remotely be connected to *class*.

Wouldn't marriage to her be perceived as a comedown?

How would she be received by his friends and family?

Had Leo thought this through?

In increasing mental agitation, Teri thought of her own family who formed the core of what little social life she had. Her father was a builder and her two brothers had also gone into trade, one a plumber, the other an electrician. They all ran successful businesses and their wives helped with the office work. They were good, down-to-earth people, open to lending a hand to anyone, giving their time freely to help her set up her restaurant. But they were no more "classy" than she was.

Her stomach started curdling as she recalled Leo had never invited her out in public with him, never introduced her to anyone. *Food and sex…*her own refrain came back to haunt her. It took considerable willpower to force it aside, arguing fiercely to herself that Leo had asked her to marry him, and other things had to be more important to him than class, like honesty and integrity. Which reminded her...

"What promises didn't your ex-wife honour?" she blurted out, her inner battle so intense she couldn't look at him this time. She fastened her gaze on the line of trees they were walking under along the sidewalk of Jersey Road, well-clipped trees for a well-kept street in "classy" Woollahra.

Leo gave a harsh little laugh. "After stringing me along for three years and conning me into buying a luxury family home, she finally told me she didn't intend to have children. Not my child nor anyone else's."

His child!

Dear God! She'd got so hung up on her own insecurities, she'd forgotten the most critical point of all!

The importance of her pregnancy to him was suddenly heart-sickeningly clear. No wonder he'd been concerned about her carrying it through, wanting repeated assurances that she didn't have a termination in mind. *She* was having the child his wife had cheated him out of and if he had to marry her to ensure his paternal rights to his son or daughter, that was what he was going to do, come hell or high water!

The chicken had come first in his other marriage.

In this one, the egg had it, never mind the chicken who was going to bear it.

"Here we are," he said, steering her towards an ornate lace ironwork gate at the end of ornate lace ironwork fence which fronted a terrace house with pristine and correct period paintwork—a recently renovated state of the art terrace house in fashionable Woollahra with a much wider frontage than most.

It shouted *money*.

It shouted *class*.

Leo opened the gate for her.

Teri paused, wondering if she should go forward. Leo certainly wanted his child in his life but what about her? She'd only been good for food and sex until now. And company, she quickly tagged on, remembering Leo's words. Undemanding company. He had *liked* being with her. But she'd been something separate from his real life, not an integral part of it. Relaxation when he needed it.

"Teri..." he prompted.

It jerked her gaze to his and her fears and uncertainties rushed off her tongue. "Am I welcome in your home, Leo? Will you hate me being there?"

CHAPTER THIRTEEN

SHE was frightened.

Leo recoiled from this view of himself. Instinctively his hand lifted and touched her cheek to soothe, to impart reassurance.

"It's okay. Of course you're welcome. We've come to see if you like it, remember?" he pressed, his mind zipping through a fast replay, seeking reasons for her fear.

She bit her bottom lip and her lashes swept down, evading his probing gaze. Defensive.

He suddenly realised that all Teri's arguments against him and what he'd laid out were defensive. Maybe it wasn't him frightening her so much as the thought of being married again, thrust into a full involvement that demanded so much more than an affair.

He wasn't overly keen on that himself, but he wasn't *frightened!* He'd deal with whatever came, one way or another. Once a choice was made, he always followed through. But maybe she was feeling trapped, being pregnant with his child. One thing he was certain of, she hadn't tried to trap him. No deceit from her, either.

"Tell me what's troubling you," he urged, wanting to fix it if he could. He slid his hand to her chin, gently tilting it up, needing a response.

"I feel...like an intruder." She raised clouded eyes to him. "This is your place. If you thought I'd fit, you'd have asked me before, Leo."

His remarks about his home...judging her by Serena's attitudes...Damn! He shouldn't have done that. Teri was different. She'd never asked him for anything. Probably because her useless ex-husband had never come good with anything. She'd simply accepted what was readily given, and if he faced the truth squarely, she'd given more than he had, letting him into her private space, always hospitable.

"It wasn't that you didn't fit," he explained earnestly, moving both his hands to her shoulders to draw her into following his reasoning. "In a way, I've been reclaiming my life after Serena got through with it, and part of that was arranging everything to suit myself. Now it's time to rearrange. And I'd rather do it with you than any other woman I've known."

She focused sharply on him. "Truly?"

He frowned at her insecurity on that point. Surely she realised...no, how could she? He'd held off too long, having had no understanding of where she'd been coming from. All the same, how he'd felt about her still held true.

"I did tell you at the beginning, finding you was like winning the lottery," he recalled, hoping to ease her concerns. "That hasn't changed."

She flushed. "That was after sex, Leo."

"No. The sex we had together affirmed it. What really got to me was...there you were, an absolute knockout, and not once did you use your body as a weapon."

"A weapon?"

He couldn't help smiling at her incredulity. "Never a sign of it, and believe me, that's rare. It's what kept me coming back...the straight give and take. If we can keep that going, I'll count myself a very lucky man to have you as my wife."

And that was a fair statement, he thought, given that he'd committed himself to marrying her.

"Lucky," she repeated dazedly, as though she found it hard to believe.

"It's true. I wouldn't lie to you," he insisted.

"No," she agreed waveringly.

"And I promise you here and now, I'll give you much more of real substance than a sweetening up box of Belgian chocolates."

She heaved a big sigh and managed a shaky little smile.

Confident that he'd beaten off the spectre of her ex-husband's failings, and determined to make Teri feel welcome in his home, he slid an arm around her shoulders and drew her through the gateway, kicking the gate shut behind them.

"You might find my furnishings a bit sparse," he warned, remembering the homely clutter of her apartment above the restaurant. "You can add stuff of your own if you like."

As long as she didn't want to change what he had, Leo thought with a twinge of uneasiness. He kept that reservation to himself as he fished the key out of his pocket. There was no point in jumping fences until they came to them. Teri might like his taste in furniture.

He opened the door and took the next step, resolved on keeping an open mind. Changes would have to be made for the baby anyway. He smiled wryly to himself. When it came right down to it, a man would do anything for his child.

CHAPTER FOURTEEN

TERI did her best to hang on to the assurances Leo had given as he ushered her into his home, but she was instantly attuned to the uneasiness behind the cheerful note in his voice.

"This slate runs through the hall, the dining room, kitchen and laundry. It's a great colour. Hardly shows any dirt."

The floor actually looked spotless, the blue-green shades in the slate glowing from a charcoal background.

"Not that it's dirty," Leo hastily added. "I have a cleaner come through once a week to keep everything right."

Of course. A cleaner. A small cost compared to what had been spent on this place. "She does a good job," Teri murmured, concentrating hard on taking in her surroundings and trying not to feel nervous about the evidence of big money. Leo apparently took it for granted. He wasn't pushing it in her face.

The hall was wide enough to accommodate a staircase as well as easy passage past it. The light from the glass panes in the front door and the window above it prevented the area from being gloomy although all the colourings were on the dark side. The wooden banister had a black lacquered finish. The stairs were covered with a thickly woven burgundy carpet. A teal wallpaper with a silky sheen covered the lower third of the walls. This was topped by a border design in teal and burgundy and white, and above it a striped wallpaper in the same colours extended to a white ceiling.

"Last house I owned was decorated in cream and pastels," Leo remarked with a telling grimace. "Nightmare of a place to live in. It was shoes off at the door in case you might soil its pristine state. No problem with that here."

"Slate is serviceable," Teri agreed, having the weird feeling he wanted her approval, though why she couldn't imagine. The fantastic quality of colour in the slate had to put it out of the range of most people's pockets.

"I reckon this wallpaper won't show grubby little fingermarks, either," he said eagerly.

"It's very classy." The comment slipped out before she could catch it back, though it wasn't a criticism and it could hardly be called an offensive remark.

"But it's vinyl. Easy to wash," he pressed.

Teri's apprehension eased. Leo seemed more concerned with practicality than class. Still, she felt it important to find out how much stylish things meant to him. "Did you choose this wallpaper yourself?"

"No. The colour scheme came with the house. It did help sell it to me, though. Everything looked touchable. Even the carpet isn't the kind to show up wine stains or other accidental spillages."

Everyone is entitled to their own sense of comfort...that was what this house was about to Leo.

Nothing more, nothing less. Everything he was saying revealed a reaction against living with an obsessively house-proud wife who had maintained a cream-and-pastel showplace without any consideration to *his comfort*.

The realisation brought a huge wave of relief to Teri. She didn't want to be afraid of touching or damaging anything, either. "It all goes so well together," she said admiringly.

"You like it then?" he asked anxiously.

"Whoever made the choices did a wonderful job."

He smiled, pleased or relieved by her response. "Same carpet and wallpaper in the lounge room," he said opening a door to their right.

She stepped in and immediately noticed that most of the wall between the lounge room and the dining room beyond it had been knocked out, opening up the whole area. A combustion heater, set against the far wall, probably warmed up the entire lower floor in winter. Her father swore by combustion heaters, always trying to persuade people to build them into their homes, but the mess of feeding wood in deterred some. Leo clearly didn't mind a bit of mess. Comfort came first.

He also fancied black leather, probably for the same practical reasons. The dining-room chairs were upholstered in it and so were a big squishy sofa and two huge armchairs, one of which was set slightly askew with a deeply cushioned footstool in front of it. Following the direction in which it was pointed, Teri glanced over her shoulder and saw a huge black television set dominating one corner of the wall that faced onto the front porch. Its screen was at least four times the size of hers.

She shook her head in amazement as she turned to get the full effect. "That must be fantastic for watching sport."

"You watch sport?"

The sharp question was instantly intimidating. Was he terribly high-brow in his choice of programs? It brought home to Teri how little they knew about each other. However, there was no point in pretence. Best to sort out their differences right now. She took a deep breath and swung to face him.

"The lot," she confessed. "Football, cricket, tennis…there's very little other conversation in my family, I'm afraid. Both my older brothers and my Dad are sport fanatics and I was brought up with all of it. Besides," She shrugged. "I enjoy it."

His face broke into a happy grin. "Great! That's another thing we share." He took her hand, his fingers threading through hers in a possessive grip that shot electric tingles up her arm. "We're going to do fine together, Teri," he declared with ringing confidence, and the champagne fizzed into her blood again.

"Come and see my table," he invited, his eyes twinkling wickedly as he drew her with him into the dining room. "I saw it in a display window and it appealed to the animal in me."

"Panthers!" she gasped in amazement.

It was a glass table. Underneath it, supporting it, were two white rocks, one with a panther and its cub sitting on it, the other with a panther climbing up it.

"It's fantastic, Leo! I love it!"

"Yeah," he drawled happily. "Only piece of furniture I've ever felt I had to have."'' He rapped the glass top with his knuckles. "This is squash court strength. Won't break. Won't mark. You just wipe everything off and it's as good as new again."

The table and eight chairs sat on a rug that was abstractly patterned in burgundy and teal and grey and pink. "I love the rug, too," Teri said with sincere enthusiasm. "It's perfect."

"I was lucky there. It was part of the display. I just bought the lot."

Teri felt a stab of envy. To feel so free with money was simply not part of her experience. She'd had to budget all her working life and most of her furniture in both the restaurant and apartment was second-hand.

"Do you do much entertaining, Leo?" she asked, gesturing at the eight chairs, still feeling wary about the social aspects of his life.

"Quite a bit, business-wise, but not here. I can't cook well enough." His eyes flirted with hers. "I reckon you could help me out with that, Teri. If you'd like."

She couldn't help laughing at him. "Maybe," she answered, her confidence lifting with his easy acceptance of her being able to partner him.

"The way you work your customers at the restaurant…you're a natural hostess," he declared admiringly.

Now he was really making her feel good. "Thank you."

Leo virtually breezed through showing her the rest of the ground floor, relaxed, genial, charming, just as he'd always been with her during their affair, and Teri found herself almost dizzy with the pleasure of it. Besides, it was a great house. There was absolutely nothing she didn't like.

The kitchen was a dream, polished green granite on the benchtops, plenty of cupboard space, every modern facility, including a large, double-sided refrigerator. Beyond that was a well-equipped laundry, a small toilet, and built onto the original structure was an extra room which Leo used as an office.

The backyard was beautifully paved with brick tiles set in a herringbone pattern and fully grown gardens along the fence; fern trees, palms, ivies, and other exotic shrubs making it a lovely leafy haven. Two dark green aluminium chairs and a matching table provided an outdoor setting for breakfast in the morning sunshine.

"I've only furnished the one bedroom upstairs," Leo informed her, the male *animal* in him simmering in very bright blue eyes as he led her back inside. "You can do what you like with the others," he added, carelessly granting her carte blanche at this point.

He was assuming she *was* going to move in here and marry him and Teri didn't correct him. She couldn't even summon up some caution. All she could think of was the bed in the bedroom and how much she wanted to be in Leo's arms again, kissing, touching, drowning in the sexual chemistry that was alive and sizzling between them, now that other issues had lost their divisive force.

Her heart was galloping as he directed her to go

ahead of him down the hall to the staircase. She felt his gaze burning through her clothes. The wanting was very definitely mutual. It seemed to thicken the very air she was trying to breathe. A tremulous excitement ran down her legs as she reached the foot of the stairs and she grabbed the banister to steady herself on the upward climb.

The doorbell rang.

Teri almost jumped out of her skin. The sound was so harsh and discordant, breaking the fine tension running between them. Her gaze jerked to Leo who'd paused adjacent to her, on the other side of the banister. He frowned at the front door, vexed by the untimeliness of the visitor.

"Expecting anyone?" Teri asked.

"No."

The bell was activated again, suggesting urgency or impatience.

"I'd better see who it is," Leo growled. His eyes flashed her a look of hot command. "Wait here. I won't be a minute."

Teri took a deep breath as he strode to the door, very much in panther mode. Leo was primed to pounce, no doubt about it. And she couldn't deny her own eagerness to be pounced upon. It had been two months since they'd last shared a bed and her whole body was tingling with anticipation, yearning for the magic Leo could weave through it.

He opened the door.

A woman fell on him.

"Thank God you're here!" she sobbed, flinging her arms around his neck, and hanging on like a clinging vine. "I didn't know where to go, who to turn to..."

"What the hell!" Leo tried to pluck her off him, then stopped, staring in shock at her face. "You've been assaulted?"

Teri couldn't see. From where she stood, a long silky fall of gleaming ash-blonde hair hid any damage.

"He hit me and hit me," the woman moaned. "And the cabbie wants to be paid. I have no money, Leo."

"Hey, mate!" a loud aggressive voice called from the street. "Are you gonna pay like the lady said...or what?"

"Be right there!" Leo shouted, then turned sharply to Teri. "Will you take her into the lounge room and sit her down while I pay the fare?"

"Sure!" she answered, though the hostile look she got from the woman whose notice was now drawn to her didn't invite help, and the moment Leo removed his support to go outside, her weak, shaken state made a remarkable recovery.

What would normally be a strikingly beautiful face was marred by an eye that was puffing up for a monster bruise and a lower lip that was split and swollen. The injuries were quite shocking and if she'd continued to weep and wail, Teri's natural kindness might have been tapped.

However, once Leo's back was turned, the woman swung her silky blonde hair over her shoulder and struck a model pose for Teri's benefit, and the rest of her showed no damage whatsoever from being mugged, apart from her mushroom pink silk blouse being unbuttoned enough and disarranged to show heaving cleavage. The figure-hugging crepe skirt in the same colour was astonishingly free of creases or smudges. The matching designer shoes were not the least bit scuffed and there didn't appear to be any runs in the smooth sheen of her stockings.

The damsel in distress, despite what pain she was feeling, eyed Teri's checked shirt and baggy jeans with distaste. "You must be the cleaner or gardener," she said snootily.

Teri fought down a flush of anger, stepping over to the lounge room door since the woman certainly didn't require *her* support in moving on her own two perfectly shod feet. "You can sit down in here," she said with an invitational wave. This was Leo's business, not hers, and she determined to stay right out of it until she learned what it was about.

But she didn't like this woman and she fiercely hated the thought that Leo was involved with her in any way. Despite the black eye in the making and the split lip, Teri's sympathy was not the least bit engaged as the woman swept past her and sailed into Leo's lounge room as though she had the right to intrude as she pleased.

Treating Teri's presence as irrelevant, she took one look at the television set and muttered, "Gross." Then her good eye fell on the heater. "Ugly." She huffed her disgust at these items and settled herself on the leather sofa, her legs gracefully disposed to show off the curve of hip and thigh, the blouse gaping seductively open.

Using her body as a weapon, Teri thought, and hoped Leo recognised it, too, since he was the one who'd given her the insight into this type of female manoeuvring. His initial reaction—to remove himself from her clutches—might have been because he was conscious of Teri witnessing it all. If he'd been alone, and not hot for sex with her...he certainly knew this woman. Which was a worry.

The drama queen tested the cushioning on the wide armrest of the sofa with her elbow, then cupped the bruised side of her face with her hand so that she looked appropriately doleful for the man she was targeting. Having set the scene to her satisfaction, she deigned to notice Teri again.

"I don't need you," she said in pettish dismissal.

"I'll just hold a watching brief," Teri said dryly.

Ignoring the baleful glare this comment evoked, she strolled past the sofa and sat down on Leo's footstool. Her gaze fell on a pile of magazines stacked on the glass-topped coffee-table beside her. *Having A Baby* was printed across the top one and underneath that caption, *Pregnancy Week By Week*. This had to be Leo's source of information.

"I said I don't need you. I want to be alone with Leo," her antagonist stated haughtily.

"He might not want to be alone with you," Teri retorted, fed up with the put-downs. She wasn't shifting until she knew what the situation was. After all, she was the invited one. Let Leo make his choice on whom he wanted with him.

"I won't discuss my private business in front of a stranger," came the next snipe.

"As far as I'm concerned, you're the stranger," Teri stated coolly.

"Which is all you know," the woman scoffed. "Leo and I go back a long way."

"I see. So you feel you can run to him for help when you get beaten up by another man."

A look of icy disdain was undoubtedly designed to freeze Teri off.

It didn't work.

She returned a look of blatant scepticism as she probed further. "Somehow I get the feeling you're not here for tea and sympathy. I take it the current boyfriend has struck out and Leo's your fallback."

"At least he's not a violent pig like Edward," she flashed out, before remembering Teri was not an appropriate person for such confidences. She immediately constructed another icy glare. "Would you please have the decency to make yourself scarce."

And leave the field free for her to climb all over Leo again? Not in a million years! The urge to torpedo this woman's act rose and fed off the snubs that had been handed out, gathering a momentum that couldn't be stopped.

"Actually," Teri drawled, "I was just about to go to bed with Leo when you interrupted. It would be much more pleasing to me if you made yourself scarce."

"In your dreams," the blonde jeered. "Leo wouldn't sink so low."

That stung. And the fact she was so sure of herself stung. "We've been lovers for the past year," Teri shot back at her, wanting to salvage her sense of superiority.

Her mouth compressed. As much as it could with a swollen lip. Her good eye glittered with malevolent fury. When she spoke it was with cutting contempt. "Do you imagine that means anything, you stupid little slut? You'll only make a fool of yourself if you do. You're completely out of his class."

"I don't think so," Teri said with more pride than belief.

"You might be a good lay but I'm the woman he married. Within three months of meeting, I might add. Now how do you measure up to that?"

For a moment, Teri's mind boggled.

This was the ex-wife?

"You're divorced!" she blurted out, recoiling from the thought that Leo had chosen this style of woman as his partner.

She smirked. "I know him so well I can correct that mistake."

Was it possible? Teri couldn't bear the thought. Yet if Serena worked on his protective instincts, made her body available, as was only too obvious...

But she wasn't pregnant with his child!

"You're too late!" Teri said in a burst of primitive satisfaction.

"Don't be absurd! I can make mincemeat of you."

"I'm having Leo's child."

"What?"

"You heard me. I'm the mother of his child. And nothing you say or do is going to change that!" She picked up the baby magazine and tossed it onto the sofa. "Read and weep, Serena."

She stared at the cover of the magazine, her smug composure cracking into ugly frustration.

"And what's more, Leo and I were planning our marriage when you so rudely interrupted," Teri stated, wanting to nail home her position in Leo's life.

Venom spat at her. "You calculating little bitch! You think you've got him. Well, let me tell you all you've got is a backlash from his marriage to me."

Footsteps in the hall.

"You're always going to live in my shadow," Serena hissed.

Leo strode into the lounge room, anger blazing from him. His vivid blue eyes lasered into Teri's. "Has she told you what this is about?"

"It's personal. Someone called Edward inflicted the damage."

"Leo, I can't go back to him," came the pitiful plea from the sofa.

He swung towards his ex-wife. "On your feet, Serena! The cab's waiting. The driver's been paid to take you wherever you want...hospital, police station, a friend's place, back to where he picked you up. I don't care. Just get out of my life and stay out!"

She rose from the sofa to a mocking provocative stance. "Such violent feelings, Leo! Nice to know you're not indifferent to me."

Having delivered her poisonous exit line she sashayed out of the lounge room, disdaining even a glance at Teri.

"I'll see that she goes," Leo said, emitting ruthless purpose as he followed her out.

A minute or two later, the front door was shut and Leo was more in control of himself when he returned. Teri hadn't moved. She felt displaced, and wondered if this was how Leo had felt when Wayne had turned up. It was not a good feeling.

"That was my ex...my very *ex*-wife," Leo informed her, grating out the words.

"Yes, I know," Teri replied quietly. "She told me."

He scanned her eyes in anxious concern. "Don't let anything she said upset you, Teri. She's a liar and a manipulator. God knows how she thought she was going to use me after all this time, but the cabbie told me she was as cool as a cucumber coming here. No tears at all."

Teri sighed to relieve the tightness in her chest. Whether Serena could have used him or not, some things she'd said had struck true. *The backlash*...this house...the opposite of a cream and pastel place, just as she was the opposite of the cream and pastel woman who'd so smugly represented a different class...and Leo tying himself to her for the sake of the child his wife wouldn't give him.

"Put her out of your mind, Teri," Leo urged, coming to take her hands and pull her off the footstool. "Let's get back to us."

The warmth he projected took some of the chill out of her mind. And there was caring in his eyes. Caring for her. She craved that from him, so much her heart was quivering from the touch of it.

"You were going to show me upstairs," she said. *The bedroom.*

The reminder brought instant ignition. Desire surged into his eyes and Teri didn't care if it was fueled by the need to wipe out Serena's disruptive visit. It was directed at her and she needed Leo to hold her, to warm her all over, to make her feel wanted for herself.

"Upstairs," he repeated. "As I said, you can have a free hand there, Teri. Come and tell me what you'd like."

Free...was there such a thing as real freedom, Teri wondered as she followed him. If she did tie herself to Leo, would she ever feel free of Serena's shadow? Could the child she was carrying make it go away?

CHAPTER FIFTEEN

IT FELT different. Right from the start it felt different. Leo, drawing her gently into his embrace, kissing her forehead, holding her close, just holding her as though he needed her warmth seeping into him, needed to feel the flesh and blood reality of her, his cheek rubbing over her hair, his mouth whispering in her ear.

"Is this okay with you, Teri?"

He'd never asked before, never shown any uncertainty over the strength of the desire coursing between them. It wasn't really a hesitation, more a caring about her feelings, beyond the physical readiness to respond.

"Yes," she answered, comforted by his embrace. It was nice just to rest her head on his broad shoulder, to breathe him in and wallow in the sense of Leo wanting to look after her.

"Just to get things straight," he murmured, "I am totally indifferent to Serena. I was angry that she came here. Angry that she even thought I could be used again. There's no way. No way at all, Teri. It's over. Like it is with you and Wayne."

"Mmmh..."

She sighed and turned her head to press her lips to the side of his neck. She didn't want to talk about his ex-wife. Nor her ex-husband. What Leo meant was it was impossible to go back. Whatever good had been there was irrecoverable. But it wasn't over. There *were* shadows, both on his side and hers. She wanted a man she could lean on, rely on. He wanted…not to be tricked.

His fingers threaded through her hair and gently tugged her head back. He kissed her, not hungrily, not passionately, more as though he was slowly relishing and deeply valuing every nuance of her openly given response. Then he tucked her head under his chin and heaved a big sigh.

"You're a great woman, Teri. And don't think I don't appreciate the person you are," he said fervently. "It's not just good sex. I've always liked being with you."

Because it had always been easy, she thought. But that time was gone, too, and it was up to them to take it from here. "I missed you," she confessed.

"Me, too. Thought of you every day. You and the baby."

His child…

"Am I holding you too tight?" He loosened his embrace. "Are your breasts still tender?"

Caring for her…

She smiled up at him. "It's okay. They're just a bit tight. I think they've got bigger."

He smiled back, bedroom mischief in his eyes. "Let me see."

With slow, teasing deliberation, he removed her shirt and bra and made his own assessment, measuring with soft circular caresses, exquisitely exciting, arousing urgent surges of need, a hot, heavy dragging feeling rushing to her loins.

"They're beautiful, Teri," he said in such a warm, loving tone, she couldn't hold back her desire for him.

"I want you, Leo. Now. Please?"

One look in her eyes and there were no more words to be said. A far more primitive communication held sway. It took only a few seconds to discard their clothes. They tumbled onto the bed, Teri wrapped her legs around him and Leo burst into her. She arched, her inner muscles gripping him possessively and into her mind came a wild pagan chant...*Mine, mine, mine...*

And the chant went on and on to the beat of his body reaching into hers. She stroked his legs with her feet, goading him into a faster, rougher rhythm. She clawed his back, digging into his skin, wanting him to belong to her so fiercely, it consumed every cell of her being. There was no room for doubts or fears about the future, no room for shadows from the past, only an overwhelming drive to seal a togetherness, a bonding that shut everything and everyone else out.

Whether Leo shared the same feeling she didn't know, but even after they'd both climaxed, he moved them into a position where he could still hold himself inside her, and when he stirred again, which happened faster than it had ever done before, he heaved her over on top of him, and his eyes glittered intense satisfaction as he watched her take her pleasure, helping her, drawing her into a wildly voluptuous indulgence of every possible sense of having him, feeling him, holding him, controlling everything until control was irretrievably lost and she collapsed onto him and there was only outside contact, heated skin against heated skin.

Still it felt wonderful with Leo clasping her close to him, kissing and fondling, and if it wasn't exactly *making love,* there was a lot to be said for this deep physical intimacy, the harmonious humming of bodies so completely sensitised to each other. The possessive pounding in her mind had stopped, but she marvelled at how strong it had been, strong and foolish. Impossible to own anyone. There was only sharing when both people wanted to. Like this.

The light from the window was fading. She smiled to herself over Leo's choice of furnishing the bedroom closest to the top of the stairs for himself rather than taking up the master suite at the front of the house. Convenience came first with him. Though he'd made it very comfortable, too, installing a queen-size bed with a lovely soft duvet and big pillows. She wouldn't mind sleeping in it. A bathroom was right next door. No problem getting to it in a hurry.

She was glad the burgundy carpet hadn't extended into the bedrooms. The light blue-grey colour in all three rooms was a nice change. And the walls were painted white. Which made it easy to furnish a nursery with pink or blue things...if she did end up marrying Leo. It would certainly give their child a lot of advantages, more than she could ever probably afford herself.

Rosy dreams, she told herself. It was all too easy to drift into them, being with Leo like this, contentedly intertwined, touching without any of the inhibitions that came into play outside the bedroom. Teri

was only too aware that what happened outside the
bedroom affected what happened inside it. Towards
the end of her marriage to Wayne, there'd been very
little desire left for any sex at all.

"Have you tried eating a dry biscuit before you get
up in the morning?" Leo suddenly asked.

"No."

He rolled her onto her back and propped himself
on his side. "It's supposed to help settle your stomach. Ginger and lemon are suggested, too," he said
seriously.

"Okay. I'll try it." A ginger snap was a dry biscuit,
one of her favourites, too, but sucking lemons was
definitely out.

Leo grinned at her and spread his hand over her
stomach. "I bet you don't even know how big he is
right now."

"He?"

"She…whatever. Our baby."

He said it so fatuously, Teri couldn't help grinning
back at him. "How big?"

"About the size of a strawberry."

"That small?" She was surprised.

"Uh-huh. But already he's got all his main organs
formed and his arms and legs are growing. His head
is becoming more erect and his neck more developed.
A tiny human being…"

His sigh was full of blissful happiness and Teri
couldn't bring herself to correct him on the gender
point again. Maybe it was just his way of talking.
After all, it didn't sound right to call their baby *it*. A

tiny human being...that image did make their child more real to her.

"There's stuff you should read up on for your own sake, Teri," Leo pressed earnestly. "Have you had a check-up with your dentist?"

"What for?"

"Well, your gums might have softened. Have they been bleeding when you clean your teeth?"

"No." She barely stifled a giggle. Leo was so unbelievably serious about all this, which was wonderful, but funny, too. Nevertheless, she didn't think he'd appreciate her amusement.

"You should make an appointment anyway." He frowned. "What about your diet? You shouldn't be touching coffee, alcohol, raw seafood or soft cheeses. No smoked salmon, either."

Teri grimaced. "I've gone off coffee. Actually I've gone off most things. I've been making do with an omelette or some soup and toast."

His frown deepened. "That won't do. You're getting thin."

"Leo, when *you* throw up half you eat, losing weight is a usual result."

"Which means we have to fix the throwing up," he said grimly. "I'm going to feed you dry biscuits and lemon and ginger every morning until this stage is over, Teri."

If he tried force-feeding her lemons, she'd throw up all over him. She arched an eyebrow, challenging his dictatorial stance. "Do you mean to keep me in this bed?"

"Best place for you," he asserted firmly.

Teri didn't really want to quarrel with that, especially if Leo was sharing the bed. Nevertheless, there were practical considerations, apart from the pleasure of having him as her lover.

"I do have a business to run," she reminded him.

He nodded. "We'll do something about that, too. Can't have you working such long hours. It's too much for you. I'll take tomorrow off work and get moving on finding someone to take some of the load off for you. Get the application forms filled out and lodged at the register office, as well."

"What application forms?"

"We'll need proof of who you are, your birth certificate, your divorce certificate..."

"Leo..." Her heart skittered at the way he was bulldozing ahead. "...I can't marry you."

He looked hard at her. "Why not? You need me to look after you, Teri."

She took a deep breath to quell the awful rise of temptation. As much as she'd like to have Leo as her husband, there was no escaping the truth or its consequences. "Because you only want to marry me for the baby," she stated baldly.

His eyebrows beetled down. "I'm sure we can make a go of it."

"Maybe," she conceded, hoping that would prove to be the case. "But it's too soon."

He thought she was quibbling and his impatience with it burst into voice. "Dammit, Teri! How can I look after you and our child properly if..."

"What if something happens, Leo?" she cut in earnestly. "Women do have miscarriages. I'm only nine weeks. If we got married and I lost your child, you'd feel tricked into a marriage you didn't really want.''

That gave him pause for thought. Nevertheless, he came back with, ''You're not tricking me, Teri. I was the one who proposed marriage.''

''I know. And I know you mean well.'' She had no doubts at all about his sincerity on that score. However, it made no difference to the crux of the matter. ''I wouldn't feel right about it, Leo. Not this early in the pregnancy.''

''Do you feel something is wrong?'' he asked anxiously.

''No. I just don't think it's a good thing to rush into marriage when there's a possibility, however remote, you won't get what you want out of it.''

''Hmmm...'' He chewed over this elemental factor. ''The danger period for a miscarriage is usually the first four months. Now I don't want any argument over this, Teri. You're moving in with me right now. We're not going to risk anything bad happening,'' he said sternly.

Her heart turned over. This child meant so much to him. She hadn't realised a man could be so wrapped up in having a child. All his reading up on it, and seeing marriage as the only way he could have full access...it would clearly be a dreadful blow if nothing came of it.

''Leo, sometimes that kind of thing is beyond anyone's control,'' she gently warned.

''That's no reason not to do our best by our kid.'' He determinedly shrugged off her fears and patted her stomach with an air of reassuring confidence. ''Don't you worry, Junior. Your Dad's taking charge. And your mother's going to do what I say because I'm the authority on your welfare.''

Despite her reservations, Teri had to smile. "If you're going to turn into a dictatorial tyrant…''

He laughed at her. "I'll reward you for good behaviour.''

"How?'' she demanded suspiciously.

"I'll let you choose the TV programs we watch.''

She rolled her eyes. "Since we both like sport…''

"I won't complain about romantic movies," he grandly offered.

"I like action movies.''

"Great!'' He looked unbearably smug.

"You're just getting your own way,'' she accused.

His eyes twinkled wickedly as he leaned over and kissed her nose. "Then I'll let you have your way with me. My body is yours. You can use me for your pleasure any time you like.''

Before she could come up with any smart retort, he covered her mouth with his and seduced her into thinking what more could she want?

Leo was intent on taking care of her and their baby and she didn't have to bear it all alone any more. He wanted her with him, in his home, in his life, in his bed. And he couldn't say she'd tricked him or tried to take him for anything. He could never say that.

She'd been absolutely fair.

As fair as she could be when she desperately wanted to keep him.

CHAPTER SIXTEEN

Two months on

DYLAN'S mother, busy cooking the bacon for the Caesar salad, looked up in surprise as Teri walked into the kitchen. "Didn't expect you to see you at the restaurant this morning," she remarked cheerily. "Aren't you having the ultrasound scan today?"

"Yes. But it's not until one-thirty. And the cleaner's at the house. And I can't stand being idle," Teri explained.

"Feeling a bit nervous about it, I expect," the older woman said knowingly.

Teri sighed. "Leo's so excited about it, Fay, I'll die if anything's wrong with this baby."

She smiled indulgently. "I'm sure there's no need to worry, dear. You've been looking so well since the morning sickness stopped. It's a good sign."

"I hope so." She'd suffered a lot of lemons to get rid of the dreaded morning sickness. In fact, she wasn't sure she could ever look another lemon in the face!

She flopped onto the stool Leo had insisted she sit on at the chopping bench and glanced down at her pot belly which wasn't so visible when she was standing. She'd replaced her red skirt with white bib and brace overalls, the red heart and smile emblazoned on

143

the bib. The elastic at the back of the waist could be
let out as she got bigger.

"At least he can't say I'm not gaining weight
now," she mockingly remarked.

Fay laughed, highly amused by Leo's fussing. All
of them—Dylan, Mel and Fay, who'd been only too
happy to accept employment with her son, taking over
much of Teri's work—had been constantly instructed
by Leo about Teri's pregnancy, what she was allowed
and not allowed to do, how she was to be watched
over and looked after, what food was good for her,
etc., etc., etc. *The Gestapo Father,* they'd christened
him behind his back. With good humour, though. It
gave them a kick to see how much he cared.

Teri swung from loving his caring, being scared by
the all-encompassing nature of it, and finding it really
exasperating when he stopped her doing things with
insidious emotional blackmail. "We've got to think
of the baby," he'd say, and then she'd feel guilty for
even feeling the occasional urge to please herself.

"Here…" Fay passed her a bowl of boiled eggs,
her eyes still sparkling with laughter. "You can shell
these. That won't hurt."

Dylan's mother was a lovely person, a widow in
her early fifties who'd been looking for employment.
She was as good-natured and as easy to get along with
as her son. A fine cook, as well, with a keen interest
in food. Leo, of course, had discovered that.

Leo had taken charge with a vengeance. Teri certainly couldn't say he wasn't as good as his word.
He'd even arranged for Dylan to take over the early
morning food buying at the markets. Everything was

working beautifully. The restaurant trade was as good as ever. Teri had never had life so easy. She had nothing to worry about.

Except having a healthy baby.

Dylan breezed in with the bread rolls from the bakery, filling the kitchen with their lovely freshly baked smell. "What are you doing here, Teri? Isn't it the scan today?"

"Yes, it is. I'm just filling in time, Dylan," she answered.

"Mel and I have bets on. I'm going for a boy and he reckons it'll be a girl."

"Dylan, Teri might not want to know which sex the baby is," Fay chided.

"How can she furnish the nursery right unless she finds out?" he argued. "That's why you're holding off doing it, isn't it, Teri?"

She shook her head. "It's too soon, Dylan. Basically I just want to know that the baby's okay."

"But you are going to see which sex it is," he pressed eagerly. "Then we can call it he or she."

"I'm sure Leo will want to know," Teri said dryly.

"Yeah." Dylan's grin was as wide as a house. "Leo won't want to miss out on knowing."

Teri was sure Dylan was right. Which was another reason she was on edge about the scan. Leo invariably called the baby *he*. Although he insisted he didn't care whether they had a boy or a girl, she suspected he would be disappointed if it was a girl and she didn't know how she was going to handle that.

It was that very question preying on her mind and playing havoc with her nervous system when she went to meet Leo at the medical centre at the appointed time. He was there before her, pacing up and down the sidewalk, exuding excitement and energy. When he spotted her coming, his face beamed such happiness at her, Teri almost fell apart. Her insides turned to mush and her legs only carried her forward because of the strong, magnetic field he threw out.

She loved this man. She really, truly did. It wasn't just fantastic sexual chemistry, though that certainly hadn't diminished. In fact, she'd never wanted nor enjoyed sex so much as she had lately. One of the plus effects of pregnancy, the magazines said, but Teri felt it was more driven by her wanting as much of Leo as she could have while everything was fine between them.

"That's such a cute outfit on you, Teri," he said as she reached him. "I was just thinking *Full Tummy—Happy Heart* applies to more than the restaurant right now." He grinned, throwing his arm around her shoulders and hugging her close. "Bet you never linked the two."

"I have actually." On the very first day she knew she was pregnant. And she'd vowed she'd have a happy heart about it no matter how Leo reacted. That wasn't quite so simple now. Her heart felt tied irrevocably to his reaction.

"Well…two great minds think alike," he said, his pleasure in the linking undimmed by her beating him to it.

He steered her up the steps leading into the medical centre, unperturbed by any doubts about the outcome of the ultrasound scan. "It'll be great having a photograph of our child," he enthused. "I mean really seeing him, not just knowing he's there. I think I'll get it framed. The first photograph."

"It may not be a he," Teri couldn't stop herself from cautioning.

"I know," Leo said blithely.

Teri tried to take comfort from this equable attitude, but once they'd been ushered into the room where the scan took place, and she was lying on the bed with her belly bare, she found it impossible to relax as the technician instructed. Leo sat on a chair beside her, holding her hand, full of happy anticipation, and that didn't help one bit.

"This gell I'll be spreading over your stomach will feel cold, but it's important for getting a good picture," the technician explained, her voice soothingly sympathetic.

Teri shivered as it was applied. Or maybe it was a shudder of apprehension.

"Now before we start, do you want to know the sex of the baby? I'll avoid that area if you prefer to keep it a surprise."

"What would you like, Teri?" Leo asked, dumbfounding her by handing her the decision.

Her immediate impulse was to put off knowing. Then everything could go on just as it had been without any sense of let-down. On the other hand, if Leo was bursting to know, he might regret giving her the choice and grow vexed with ignorance. Unsure which was the better course, Teri gave up on it.

"You decide, Leo."

"Hmmm...." He seemed in two minds, his head

cocking from side to side, obviously tempted yet...Teri could hardly believe her ears when he said, "Let's leave it as a surprise." His eyes danced at her. "I have this fantasy of the doctor handing me our baby and saying, 'Mr. Kingston, you have a...whatever.' It won't be such a big moment if I know already."

Teri laughed in sheer relief. It surely meant he really didn't mind if it was a son or a daughter. She turned to the technician, smiling her agreement. "That's it then. We don't want to know."

"Fine. I'm switching off the overhead light now so you get a better view on the monitor. Just watch the screen and I'll describe what I'm checking."

The monitor screen hung above the foot of the bed. Leo squeezed her hand as the room was plunged into darkness. Teri held her breath and fiercely prayed for everything to be normal. Then the screen lit up and there was her baby...recognisably a baby...head, neck, body, arms, legs, little feet tucked in. It was amazing, incredible, awesome.

The technician moved a dot around the screen, pointing out the heart, the spinal cord, and various other features that were simply a blur to Teri. What she saw was a tiny person with a nose and ears and chin and mouth, and unbelievably, as the technician clearly showed, he or she was sucking its thumb and the sucking motion was actually visible.

"The progression is precisely what it ought to be at eighteen weeks," the technician assured them.

Magic words to Teri.

Suddenly, the curled little hand attached to the sucked thumb opened up into a four-finger fan.

"Look, Teri! He's waving to us!" Leo cried excitedly. "He knows we're looking at him and he's waving to us."

True or not, it was so wonderful, tears welled into her eyes. Their baby...saying hello, telling them he was fine in his mummy's tummy and they weren't to worry about him.

"Isn't he great?" Leo said huskily, *his* fingers squeezing hers so hard they were almost pulped, but Teri didn't care. As a sharing moment, this had to be the most heart-moving in her whole life.

She was still treasuring it after the scan, while she redressed herself, and all the way out to the street where the afternoon sunshine added its sparkle to her glow of happiness.

And right there on the public sidewalk Leo turned her into his embrace and hugged her as though she was the most precious thing in the world to him.

"I can never thank you enough for giving me this, Teri," he said fervently. "It's so special..."

"Yes, it is," she whispered, her throat choked with emotion.

"I might have missed it, but for you." He heaved a deep sigh and eased back a bit, his eyes seeking hers, their irises a brighter blue than she'd ever seen them. "You have to marry me, Teri. It's the right thing to do. We made that baby. You and I, together. We're his Mum and Dad."

His voice was furred with deep feeling and she understood the emotions swirling through him. She was completely in tune with what he was saying. But it was their child...the image of a tiny hand waving to them...driving what he felt.

"This isn't the time, Leo," she said quietly.

"Yes, it is," he pressed with intense urgency. "I want to be married to you. We're a family, Teri...don't you see?"

"Not yet, Leo. When our baby's safely born. Then we'll be a family."

"But he's real now."

"Yes. But he couldn't survive by himself at this point. Let him be born, Leo, alive and yelling and kicking. When the doctor puts him in your arms and says, 'Mr. Kingston, you have a...whatever,' if you still want to marry me, ask me then."

"No." His eyebrows beetled down, lending a deep angst to his expression. "I want us to be married before he's born. He'll be illegitimate if we're not."

She shook her head. "That's not a social stigma anymore."

"You've been happy with me, haven't you?" he pressed, determined on persuasion. "It's been good, sharing our lives. I like coming home to you. It seems to me we've got it together better than most people, Teri."

"The baby gives us a common purpose," she gently reminded him.

"Exactly. So..."

Unable to bear any more, she reached up and placed her fingers on his lips. "Please...let it go for now, Leo. Please?"

He struggled with his own strong inclinations. "It's wrong," he said gruffly.

"No. It can wait," she corrected him as firmly as she could with her own emotions torn by caution. "I want to thank you, too, for giving me a wonderful memory today. I'll always hug it in my mind. Always." Tears pricked her eyes. "I'm going back to work now. Okay? I'll see you tonight."

She broke away from him before he could stop her and strode blindly along the sidewalk, her heart pumping madly. She half expected him to catch up with her and pursue his argument but he didn't. For which she was profoundly grateful. The tears would not be blinked away. They kept swimming into her eyes.

She'd wanted so much to say yes to his proposal this time.

But she couldn't.

It was wonderful that everything was fine with the baby. Even so, that was no guarantee she would carry it full-term without mishap. There were so many things that could go wrong. She'd read about them—awful lists of problems—in the magazines Leo had bought. And only a week ago, she'd watched a TV program where a healthy baby strangled itself on its cord when it turned around, just before it was due to be born.

If she lost Leo's child, the grief would be terrible. It would tear them apart. She knew it would. Only love could hold a couple together through such a terrible loss. And Leo didn't love her. Not for herself.

He only loved her because she was carrying his child. He would never have asked her to marry him otherwise. That was the truth of it and it was no use trying to fool herself otherwise.

CHAPTER SEVENTEEN

LEO could not get back into work. Useless trying, he decided. He'd been staring blankly at the monitor screen on his PC for the past hour, alternatively exulting over the fantastic image of his child in Teri's womb, and suffering considerable heartburn over her refusal to marry him. There was no reason to it that he could see. Which probably meant it was some female thing he didn't understand.

Disgruntled at not being able to figure out how to change Teri's mind, and not prepared to accept failure on this vital point, Leo did what he probably should have done in the first place instead of pummelling his male brain with questions that had no rational answers. He pressed the button on the intercom to summon assistance.

"Mavis, I need you in here."

He pushed away from his desk and stood up, lacking a sense of authority on this thorny subject and wanting to feel he was at least in charge of his office. Mavis came in and he waved her to the chair she usually occupied during work discussions. She settled herself and looked inquiringly at him.

He wandered around his desk and propped himself against it, determined to stay relaxed and reasonable, no matter what advice Mavis gave. After all, she had been right about the pregnancy causing Teri to get completely screwed up in her responses to him.

"This is a personal problem, Mavis," he stated to get her mind set in the right direction.

"Ah!" she said, the bright expectancy in her eyes wavering into wary reserve.

"You know I got Teri to move in with me."

She nodded.

"That was two months ago," he emphasised so his trusty assistant was clear on the time factor.

Another nod.

He proceeded to apprise her of the situation. "I've given Teri every consideration, listened to her needs and acted on them, eased her work situation so she gets plenty of rest, done everything I can to take care of her. In short, I've carried through precisely what you said to do."

Mavis apparently didn't see fit to comment on his thoroughness. Her eyes seemed to be weighing his words.

Leo couldn't think of anything he'd overlooked. He frowned over the sheer perversity of Teri's attitude. "She and I get along very well, Mavis. We don't have any of those picky arguments. We even like the same programs on TV. And there's certainly no problem with...uh..." He really didn't want to go into their sex life.

Mavis gave him an arch look. "I take it you mean you're happy together."

"Yes," Leo seized gratefully.

"And you love each other."

Leo felt an instant recoil to that power-laden word.

It held so many blackmail connotations from Serena's use of it, to attach it to any good relationship was tantamount to spoiling it. Teri evoked feelings in him that Serena never had. Never. From the very beginning it had been completely different with Teri. And now that he'd shown her he wasn't another Wayne...yes, this was the *real* thing. And the sharing was too good for the feelings not to be mutual.

"No problem there, Mavis," he firmly assured her. "And that's why this doesn't make sense. There we were at the ultrasound scan earlier this afternoon, both of us over the moon at seeing our baby. It was the perfect moment to ask Teri to marry me so I did. But she refused to consider it. Flatly refused. Now I ask you..." He spread his hands in appeal. "...why would she turn me down?"

"Did she say why?" Mavis asked cautiously.

Leo threw up his hands in perplexity. "Only that it's too soon. She said to ask her again after the baby's born, but that will be too late, Mavis."

"Too late for what?"

He grimaced. "Teri says it doesn't matter if our child is illegitimate, but I really don't like it. How will it be, Teri going into hospital under her own name and having our baby as though it has nothing to do with me. It's like she's cutting me out."

"But she hasn't really cut you out of anything so far, Leo," Mavis pointed out with her usual perspicacity.

It didn't settle his disgruntlement. "Why can't she marry me?" he demanded, wanting a direct reply.

"There could be many reasons," Mavis mused.

"Like what?"

"Some expressions of love count more than others, Leo," she said, her eyes gathering a distant look as though seeing much further than he could. "Have you met her family?" she asked speculatively.

"No." He frowned over the question. "Surely this is between me and Teri?"

"Has she met yours?"

He shrugged. "There's only Dad and he's tied up with his second family now. I don't see much of them myself since he moved down to the South Coast."

"So you've asked Teri to marry you, but neither of you have involved each other with your families," Mavis said, as though he'd missed something critically important.

"We're starting our own family," Leo argued.

"Is it your plan to leave them out of your wedding?"

"Oh, for God's sake, Mavis!" He rolled his eyes at such an irrelevant issue. "Teri and I are both divorced. We've been through the wedding rigmarole before. A register office ceremony will do fine. It's just a matter of getting married."

"You know this is how she feels?"

"We haven't got as far as talking about it," he said tersely.

"I see," she said, going into her wise nodding act. "Then you're telling me that what you want from Teri is a piece of legal paper to give you legal rights over your child. Have I got that right?"

"Well…yes. Though it's a commitment to our future together, too."

"If you mean to make a future together, I don't think you can ignore your families," she advised. "To my mind, that is elemental. They're part of you. Part of your life. There's more than a baby involved in a marriage, Leo. I think your Teri is very aware of that."

Leo mulled over this bigger picture. "So you think I should win approval from her family." It should be easy, he thought. He could talk sport to her father and brothers.

"I would imagine Teri would like to feel your family's approval, too," Mavis added pointedly.

Leo smiled, happily confident with this course of action. "No problem with Dad," he said with absolute assurance. "He'll think she's terrific after Serena."

"Then it could be a good move to set up meetings on both sides and start building a broader base for the future."

Leo could see the sense in forging some allies in the marriage stakes. "Thank you, Mavis," he said with satisfaction. "You reckon that will do the trick."

"Oh no!" she cried, shaking her head emphatically. "I very much doubt anything will do the trick."

That straightened him up with a jolt. "Then what's the use of what you've just told me?"

"It may give you a better chance of having your proposal accepted *after* the baby is born."

"Mavis." He eyed her sternly. "The whole purpose of this conversation is to change Teri's mind *before* the birth."

She didn't bat an eyelash, holding his gaze and

squarely returning it as she replied, "Well, Leo, if you want my opinion, you've got no chance of that happening and you may very well alienate Teri if you keep trying. She *said* after. And that was at the perfect moment. My advice is to work towards the next perfect moment, which may possibly be when you lay your child in her arms after the birth."

Leo's eyebrows beetled down in brooding frustration. It was uncanny her hitting precisely on what Teri had said. Women—even well-earthed Mavis—had a logic of their own that a man simply wasn't privy to. Except it wasn't *logic* at all.

"You can't suggest anything else?" he pleaded, hating having to accept defeat.

She stood up, preparing to go, having delivered her woman's wisdom. She paused a moment, cocked her head on one side, and said, "I really wouldn't press for your practical piece of legal paper. It has no soul."

"Soul?" he repeated, finding the word too nebulous to pin down.

"Soul," she affirmed, her eyes accusing him of being very thick as she turned to make her exit from his office.

No point in calling her back. Mavis had clearly had the last word. Leo brooded over it all for a long time. Eventually he came to two conclusions. He'd better follow his assistant's advice, and when he did ask Teri to marry him again, *after the birth*, he'd invite her to say how she'd like them to get married so he didn't get it wrong with the register office.

Maybe then he'd understand *soul*.

CHAPTER EIGHTEEN

TERI knew there was no hiding her pregnancy from her family any longer. The excuses she'd made not to visit over the past couple of months could not be extended forever, especially since they lived at Bateau Bay, only a two-hour drive away. Now that the scan had assured her a miscarriage was unlikely, she really did have to face up to the inquisition that was bound to follow breaking the news.

Nevertheless, she kept putting it off day after day, unsure if she should involve Leo or not. To her astonishment, he himself broached the subject one night over dinner.

"I called my dad today," he said, shooting her a dazzling smile. "Told him he was going to be a grandfather. He wants to meet you, Teri. He and his wife and my two half-brothers live down the South Coast at Kiama. We could go this Sunday if that's okay with you."

It was the first she'd heard of Leo's family. Apart from saying there were no girls in it, she knew nothing of his background. Having been handed the opportunity to probe a little, she did, finding out his mother had died when he was eight and his father, a professional accountant, had remarried when Leo was in his teens at boarding school.

"I usually visit them at Easter and Christmas," he

explained. ''The boys are still young enough to enjoy getting Easter eggs and presents from me.'' He lifted his eyebrows appealingly. ''I hope you don't mind my telling them about the baby.''

''No. I'd like to visit,'' she answered truthfully, curious to know more. ''It's nice that you get on with them. I mean your father's second family.''

''What about your family, Teri?'' He frowned. ''I don't know what you've told them, but I'd like the chance to assure them I mean to look after you and our child.''

She sighed in sheer relief. ''It would help.''

''Help?'' he picked up quizzically.

She winced. ''They live on the Central Coast and they don't know about the baby yet. I've been wimping out on it. I knew they'd want to meet you and I wasn't sure...''

He reached across the table and covered her hand with his, instantly causing her pulse to leap and her skin to heat. Her mind floundered momentarily, her thought patterns jammed by the intense flow of magnetic energy Leo poured forth.

''Teri, I'll back you up on anything,'' he said, his vivid blue eyes ablaze with promise. ''Just make a day for visiting them and you can be absolutely sure of my support.''

''Oh!''

She was lost for words. Tears pricked her eyes. Her heart thumped so hard it hurt her chest. Surely this meant he cared about her, standing by her in front of her parents, ready to deflect any critical remarks and shoulder responsibility. She swallowed hard, trying to hold on to some composure.

"My parents are…well, rather old-fashioned," she warned. "And my brothers' marriages are solid. None of them ever really understood why Wayne and I broke up. It won't be easy, Leo."

There was not the slightest sign of faltering from him. "We'll take it as it comes, Teri." He squeezed her hand. "The sooner they see how good we are together, the better."

"You really don't mind?" she had to ask, hardly able to bring herself to believe he was willing to commit himself so far on her behalf. "They'll probably give you the third degree," she added apprehensively. "My father, in particular, is not known for his tact."

"Don't worry. I'll handle it. They're not about to turn their backs on our child, Teri."

Our child

It was like a douche of cold water on fevered hopes. Leo didn't love her. Everything he did to ease her life was really for their precious child. The core of their one-on-one relationship was what they shared in bed. Always had been and probably always would be.

Still, she had nothing to complain about. He was good to her. He took care of things with a generosity that invariably made her feel mean to even wish for more from him. She loved him. She just found it increasingly painful that he didn't love her and there was nothing she could do about it.

The following Sunday they drove down to Kiama with Leo assuring her of a warm welcome. Which proved to be true. Jim Kingston looked like an older version of Leo, and had the knack of giving kindly attention, putting her at ease. His wife, Donna, a vivacious redhead who clearly adored her older husband, talked so much herself she never allowed an awkward moment to develop. It turned out they were both highly relieved Teri was nothing like Serena.

"Such a cold, calculating woman," Donna confided. "It's obvious Leo is much happier with you, Teri. And it's such lovely news about the baby."

Her warm smile did a lot to diminish Serena's classy shadow. So did their home which was totally unpretentious—a large, sprawling weatherboard house with wide verandahs, set right on the edge of the beach. It was very much a family house, with Leo's two younger half-brothers having the run of it as they pleased, both of them bright, happy boys who constantly wanted Leo to play with them. Which he did.

"He'll make a good father," Jim Kingston assured her. "I'm glad he's got you and the baby in his life now. Leo got too caught up in making money. He needs to slow down. There's more to life than money and what it can buy. That first wife of his..." He grimaced and patted Teri's hand. "A pleasure to meet you, my dear. A real pleasure."

Leo hadn't slowed down much, Teri thought, but maybe he would after the baby was born. *If* all went well with the birth.

The visit could certainly be counted a success. Not only was it nice to have Jim's and Donna's approval, but Teri felt more comfortable about taking Leo into the midst of her family. He hadn't come from a snobby background. She thought—hoped—he would fit in with the same charming ease he invariably displayed wherever he was.

With the confidence of knowing Leo would stand by her, Teri finally screwed up her courage to confess her situation to her mother over the telephone, determined on answering all the tricky questions so that the shock factor, at least, was taken out of the face to face meeting when she and Leo turned up.

There were tears and recriminations and a great deal of talk of *"for the sake of the child,"* with Teri finally losing patience and shouting she didn't believe in shotgun marriages and no one was going to drive her into one and she certainly didn't need the stress of being made to feel guilty, or be put before a family jury telling her what she should do with *her* future. At which point she slammed the telephone down and dissolved into a flood of tears herself.

That night she told Leo he could forget about meeting her family, and proceeded to cry herself to sleep. The next morning, he told her he'd talked to her parents himself and had invited them to come down to Woollahra and have lunch with both of them at his home this coming Sunday, and if Teri was agreeable, she should call her mother and let her know.

Teri instantly flared with angry suspicion. "Leo, if you told them you're going to marry me…"

"You know I can't do that without your consent, Teri," he cut in, appealing to reason. "I merely said you were extremely distressed and were in a very delicate condition, being in the second trimester of pregnancy, and if they cared about you and the grandchild you're carrying, they'd give you every support instead of upsetting you.''

Of course. Nothing—absolutely nothing!—was to put at risk the safety of his child. Mr. Fix-it in action again. She almost hated him at that moment. Though when she did call her mother who was apologetic and anxious to smooth over everything, Teri had to acknowledge she was grateful for Leo's intervention, despite the awful jealousy she felt towards the baby he cared so much about. Her family meant a lot to her. She didn't want to feel at odds with them.

Her parents duly landed on the doorstep of Leo's home in Jersey Road. They were highly impressed by Leo and everything to do with Leo, even the panther table. They departed in the warm belief their daughter was *in good hands*. Which she was. Teri readily conceded it was so. Though it almost choked her.

It was the baby in good hands...the baby...the baby...the baby!

It was a struggle to keep herself on an even keel and not get neurotic about it. Leo was kind and considerate. He was very loving in bed, especially tender as she got bigger and bigger. He massaged her tight shoulders, rubbed her aching back, and worked oil into her skin, easing the itch of its stretching. When he insisted on going shopping with her for the baby, Teri knew it would be downright mean to put him off.

She selected basic nursery furniture and a few baby clothes, hoping she wasn't jinxing herself by this substantial assumption that nothing would go wrong with the baby.

He blithely bought a colourful array of wall hangings, falling in love with Pooh Bear and Piglet and Tigger. Teri had to drag him out of the soft toy department, but not without an armful of animals he fancied. Then he became entranced with mobiles of tropical fish and a moon with stars revolving around it.

To Teri, the whole nursery business was like a tempting Fate exercise. It represented expectations on a scale that kept growing and growing with every purchase Leo made. She wished he'd stop but she couldn't bring herself to spoil his pleasure.

She also nursed a gnawing wish he would buy her something, just especially for her, even if it was only because she was the mother of his child. He didn't think of it and it was undoubtedly unreasonable of her to want him to. After all, she hadn't bought him anything for being the father of her child.

Her fears about her pregnancy lessened as it stayed trouble-free through the last trimester. She bloomed. Everyone commented on it. And the baby moved around so much, Teri dubbed it "the ice-skater." It really was fascinating to see and feel a foot sweep across her stomach. Leo was enchanted by it.

Her mother called frequently to check on progress and give helpful advice. Leo met her brothers and their families. Despite their long friendship with Wayne, her brothers were favourably impressed by Teri's "new man." There was no sport Leo couldn't discuss with them and it was obvious he was devoted to Teri's welfare.

The waiting time grew shorter. Leo took her to the ante-natal classes at the hospital where he'd booked a private room for her. In one session they were shown a video of natural childbirth. Teri found it so scary, she didn't want to know any more. She went to the breathing lessons in the hope they might help her through what she'd seen, but flatly refused to go to the video of a Caesarian operation.

Leo went. He wanted to be prepared for all possibilities. Naturally. Anything that might affect *his child* had to be known, never mind what Teri had to go through to deliver it.

The due birth date finally came.

And went.

The waiting was dreadful. She stopped going to the restaurant, unable to bear the sympathy and continual inquiries, and the fussing. Each day Leo kept asking if she felt any symptom of labour, and Teri had to bite her tongue lest she snap his head off.

The doctor assured her the baby was in the right position, ready to come, but nothing was happening. She was as big as a whale. She couldn't see her feet. And all Leo could think of was the imminent birth of his child. The doctor promised that if she went five days overdue, he would induce the birth.

At eight o'clock on the night of the fifth day she went into hospital. A gell was applied to get things moving. Teri did as she was told and lay still for a couple of hours to give the gell every chance to do its work, but as far as she could tell, it was having no effect at all.

Leo had turned on the TV in the room and was

watching the Friday Night Football Match. She was supposed to be watching, too, to help pass the time. It was impossible for her to concentrate on the game and she had no idea who won. When it was over, Leo switched the set off and looked hopefully at her.

"Nothing," she replied dolefully. "I don't think this baby wants to be born."

"Just a matter of time, Teri," he assured her, excited anticipation in his eyes. "You're here in the delivery ward. It's going to happen."

The midwife they'd met in the ante-natal classes came in to check on her. "Any action?"

"Not a twinge," Teri said flatly.

"Then I suggest you settle down for the night and try to get some sleep. It's quite usual in these cases for labour not to start until morning and I wouldn't expect the baby to be born before late tomorrow afternoon."

A whole day of labour! Teri quailed at the thought.

The midwife turned to Leo. "You'd best go home to bed and try to sleep, too. You won't be any help to your partner if you're too fatigued to concentrate when it counts."

Leo frowned. "I don't like leaving Teri alone. What if it starts earlier?"

"We'll call you," the midwife assured him. "It is best that you go. Teri will be more likely to sleep without you here."

No, I won't, Teri thought, panic fluttering through her mind. She didn't want to be left alone. Tonight of all nights she needed Leo beside her. She was frightened of tomorrow.

"I guess it is the sensible thing to do," he said, reluctantly rising from the chair next to her bed.

No...no...stay! Teri screamed in her mind, fiercely willing him not to do the sensible thing this once! She wanted to tell him how she felt, plead...but she knew how he would reply. The birth would go better if she was properly rested. The baby would need her help tomorrow.

He leaned over and gave her a gentle good-night kiss. Her eyes ached with silent begging as he stroked her hair away from her face and smiled happy reassurance. "We'll be holding him this time tomorrow, Teri," he said. "Isn't that a sweet dream to have?"

She couldn't even imagine it. A long dark, lonely night loomed ahead of her. "Don't go," she croaked, fear choking her throat.

He hesitated, then grimaced appealingly. "The sooner I go, the sooner you'll get to sleep. Don't worry. I'll be here like a shot if I get a call."

"I know," she sighed, resigning herself to the inevitable. Though a spurt of rebellion made her mutter, "I don't feel like being sensible."

"Neither do I," he confessed, and kissed her again, causing her heart to flutter with hope. Then he murmured, "Try to have a good night's sleep, Teri."

After which he did the sensible thing.

He left.

And Teri didn't sleep a wink.

She decided she hated Leo, hated the baby, and hated herself for ever being such a fool as to think she would be happy to become a mother.

CHAPTER NINETEEN

LEO hated having to leave Teri. He forced himself to do it for her sake. She hadn't slept much last night, too uncomfortable to settle properly and fretful about the baby not coming. The labour would be more of an ordeal for her if she didn't get some good rest.

He knew she was frightened of what lay ahead. The video on natural childbirth had been too graphic. He wished she hadn't watched it. It was all right for him since he needed to know how best to help her, but he wasn't looking forward to seeing Teri in pain. He hoped it wouldn't be for too long.

The drive home from the hospital was only ten minutes. He parked the car in the street rather than garage it at the back of the house. A quick getaway was essential if he was called. Determined on being properly rested himself, Leo had a hot shower and went straight to bed. He applied every relaxation technique he knew and eventually dropped off to sleep.

The shrill ring of the telephone woke him. It was pitch dark. He fumbled for the receiver, bleary eyes targeting the digital clock next to the phone—2:47. So soon? Was something wrong? "Yes?" he barked at the caller, anxiety squeezing his heart.

"Mr. Kingston?"

"Yes!" he snapped impatiently.

"This is Nurse Williams calling to let you know Miss Adams is already in advanced labour."

"Advanced?" he shouted, appalled at having been left in ignorance. Teri, doing it alone…

"It's come on quickly," the nurse explained.

Leo slammed down the receiver and hurtled out of bed. He pulled on essential clothes at the speed of light, grabbed his keys and wallet and was off, savagely castigating himself as he raced down the stairs and out to his car. He shouldn't have left her. He should have sat by her every minute. He should have known the damned hospital staff couldn't be trusted to watch over her as he would have done, ready to be supportive and reassuring.

The streets were virtually deserted and he made it to the hospital in seven minutes. The elevator to the delivery ward was so slow he could barely control his frustration. Once it opened on the right floor, he sprinted down the corridor and burst into the room they'd put Teri in.

The bed was empty!

No-o-o-o, his mind screamed. Not yet. She couldn't have the baby without him.

He was about to yell for someone when his ears registered the ensuite shower running. The door was open. He looked in and there she was, slumped back on a white plastic chair, her eyes shut, one hand managing a manual shower spray which was shooting hot water over her stomach while she gingerly rubbed the tight mound.

For a moment, Leo was overwhelmed by the sheer beauty of her naked, the epitome of womanhood, large dark nipples and aureoles adorning her magnificent breasts, her smoothly distended abdomen full with child, lovely long legs in an ungainly sprawl that was somehow deeply endearing.

His heart swelled with his feeling for her. He wished he could photograph her just like this, keep this image of her forever, and the reminder of all she was to him...the woman who touched him in ways no other did, somehow fulfilling him as a man, giving him his child and so much more. So much...

Then her head tilted back and a tortured moan spilled from her throat.

"Teri..." Her name ripped from his. "I'm here, love. Tell me what you want."

Her eyes flew open, huge and hopelessly woebegone. "It's horrible, Leo," she wailed.

"I know, I know," he tried to soothe.

"You don't know," she cried. "It's not you suffering this...this...o-o-oh!" She bent forward, huddling over the pain of the contraction.

He crouched beside her. "Let me do the shower spray," he offered anxiously.

"I want pethidine," she sobbed. "Bad pain. Bad...bad pain."

"Nurse! Nurse!" Leo yelled, agitated by his own helplessness.

A woman came running in. "What is it?"

"Teri needs pethidine."

"Well, let's get her out of the shower and into the delivery room. Then I'll call the midwife."

It was a dreadful business, getting Teri dried and into a hospital gown. She kept doubling up and begging for pain relief. Leo assured her again and again it would be administered as soon as possible. But when they got her into the delivery room and the midwife examined her, it was too late for the pethidine. The baby was on its way and there wouldn't be time for it to work. It was better to concentrate on riding out the birth now.

"Riding!" Teri shrieked between panting for breath. "Are…you…crazy?"

"I'll go and call the doctor," the midwife said.

"Tell him…tell him not to…not to put a tie on. Hurry…"

"Roll onto your side, Teri," Leo urged. "I'll rub your back."

"You weren't here," she sobbed.

"I'm sorry, love. I'll try to make up for it now," he promised, easing her onto her side as gently as he could.

"Don't call me love," she moaned. "You don't love me. Oh God!…oh, God!…please let me die.…"

Leo got his hand working in circular caresses on her lower back and leaned over to kiss her ear. "I do love you, Teri. You know I do. And I'd hate it if you died on me. Now be a good girl and concentrate on breathing the way…"

"Only saying that to make me…oooh!" Her legs writhed up. "Never loved me," she sobbed. "Only the baby."

"That's not true."

"'Tis true."

It had to be the pain talking. She had to know in her heart how much she meant to him. "Teri, you're the best thing that ever happened to me," he declared fervently, disturbed by the flow of negative feelings.

"'Cause o' the baby," she cried accusingly.

"No!" She had it wrong. Wrong from the start. Damn Serena for screwing him up on the *love* word. If Teri needed to hear it...Damn, damn, damn! This was his fault and he had to correct it, had to make her understand. Here she was, having his child, and she didn't think he loved her?

"Before you say it was only ever sex," he blurted out, "it was always more than that, Teri. I just didn't realise how much you meant to me until you threw me out in favour of your ex-husband."

"You didn't...come back," she jeered through another agonised groan.

"So I had my nose out of joint," he readily confessed. "And I didn't want to admit you were important to me. I told myself I had to check on my child. But, Teri, it was *you* having my child that finally drove me back."

"Don't b'lieve you," she gasped.

"I swear to God! I love sharing my life with you."

"Never said." Her voice rose in a high-pitched scream, then choked into, "Never...never...said," as she burst into tears.

"I did say," he insisted anxiously. "After the scan I told you how I felt."

"Didn't love me," she sobbed.

"Dammit, Teri! I did. I do. Ask my father. Ask your parents. They know I love you. I went into battle for you and let both your mother and father know in no uncertain terms that they didn't know what love was if they let you down when you were feeling so frightened and unsure of everything. And I told 'em it was all that bastard, Wayne's fault.''

"Way-ayne?" The name shuddered out of her.

"That's right. Him! Messing you up so you were scared of counting on anyone. That guy never loved anyone except himself. You'd better believe it," he said fiercely.

She curled up again, desperately panting. "You... married S'rena...on'y three months..."

"Blind fool that I was." He rubbed her back frantically, uncaring that his own back was aching from leaning over to help her. "I'm more married to you than I ever was to her," he asserted as the contraction eased. "And we would have been married legally if you'd let me."

"Give...child...your name," she cried in wretched misery.

"And you, Teri. You," he repeated emphatically, needing to get through to her, hating the fact that she had felt so insecure with him. "But you wouldn't have me," he explained, "and Mavis advised no pressure, to wait until after the baby."

"Who...May...vis?" Such awful laboured sounds.

"She works for me. Good woman. Knows I'm besotted with you. Can't work half the time for thinking of you."

"'Sotted?" It came out weak and quavery.

"I've tried to think of everything...everything...to keep you with me and make you see you can trust me, Teri. I'm here for you because I want to be here

for you. If that's not love I don't know what love is,"
he cried in sheer desperation.

"Not...baby?"

The quivering uncertainty killed him. "The baby,
too, because he's part of you, part of me, part of us,"
he pressed with passionate intensity. "But even if
there was no baby, I love you, Teri. It's like...you've
made a new world for me and it's good. It's so unbelievably good."

"Yes..." It was barely a hiss ahead of a long anguished moan. "I can't stand it, Leo. Make them stop
it. Make them...oh, ple-e-e-ease!"

"We need help in here!" he bellowed.

The midwife strode in accompanied by a nurse.
"Doctor's on his way. We're going to administer gas,
Teri. It will help the pain and regulate your
breathing."

"Thank God for that!" Leo muttered.

"Deep breath in," the nurse instructed. "Now
breathe out hard enough to make it rattle. Good girl.
Breathe in again..."

"Head's engaged," the midwife informed them.
"You'll feel like bearing down soon."

Teri was sucking in gas so hard, Leo wasn't sure
she'd heard. The nurse was getting her into a steady
breathing rhthym. He'd been no use at all with the
process they'd learnt together. He kept rubbing her
back, hoping it helped, hoping what he'd said had
helped, too. It appalled him that he'd left her lying in
the dark, believing he didn't love her, thinking he
only cared about the baby. What more could he have
done to have shown her? Did she believe him now?

A groan of sheer anguish rattled his nerves. Teri rolled onto her back, the gas violently discarded. He grabbed her hand. Her fingers dug into his like talons as she lurched forward. He quickly slipped his arm around her shoulders, hugging her supportively. His heart was hammering.

"Go with the need to push, Teri," the midwife instructed, "but not too hard all at once."

The doctor made his entrance. "Ah...on its way," he said with satisfaction.

Suddenly it was all action. Leo remembered Teri wasn't supposed to give birth on her back but there was no time to change position. Nothing was going to plan. The hospital gown was drawn up out of the way. Instructions and encouragement were being called out. Teri was frantically trying to follow orders. Leo heard himself echoing what everyone else was saying, wildly anxious for it to be over for Teri's sake.

Then a tiny red and purple and white and black body seemed to rush into the doctor's hands and the distinctive cry of a newborn baby silenced all of them. Teri flopped back onto the pillow exhausted.

"It's okay," he murmured, stroking her damp hair away from her damp forehead. "It's born. It's over. And I love you more than I can ever say."

She smiled weakly at him. "What is it, Leo?"

He dragged himself away from her. The baby was being wiped and yelling its dislike of the outside world. "What have we got, Doctor?" Leo asked.

"Mr. Kingston, you have a fine, healthy daughter."

And the baby was placed in his arms.

"A daughter," Leo repeated in wonderment. He carried the baby back to Teri and carefully laid it across her bare tummy, just under her breasts. "We've got a little girl, Teri."

"Oh, Leo! Look at her hair! It's so black and so thick!" She touched the baby lovingly, then lifted big shiny eyes to him. "Do you mind that it's a girl?"

"Mind? I think it's marvellous. I could have done boy things with a boy, but a girl...she's going to show me a whole new world. Like you, Teri. Only this will be from the beginning and I'm going to love every minute of it."

Tears welled into her eyes. "I love you, too, Leo. I'm sorry I couldn't see past the baby."

He lifted one of her hands and kissed it. "Just say you'll marry me, Teri."

"I will. I'll be happy to, Leo. Very happy."

He sighed, his heart overflowing with relief and joy. The baby gave a funny, high-pitched little squeal, as though testing her voice again and they laughed, exhilarated by the new life they would share together. Then their eyes met and locked and the good feeling flowing between them went deep. Deeper than ever before. No barriers. No shadows. A pure shaft of glorious feeling.

It was a moment Leo would never forget.

The most perfect moment.

It had *soul*...open, loving, giving to each other.

And Leo's understanding of that word was complete.

CHAPTER TWENTY

TERI woke sluggishly, feeling muddled as to whether she wanted to open her eyes or not, yet there was something important swirling around the back of her mind, some sixth sense telling her it was good to wake up even though she was still tired.

Her hand automatically drifted to her tummy, a soft, spongy, deflated tummy, and the connection clicked. The baby! She'd had the baby! And it was a girl!

Her eyes opened in a flash. She was in the private room Leo had booked for her and broad daylight was streaming through the wall-long picture window. Along its ledge were baskets and bowls of lovely flowers, an abundance of pink roses and carnations. Who had sent them? And so soon?

Her gaze swung around the room, but there was no hospital bassinet. Then she remembered the nurse wheeling it away, saying they'd keep the baby in the nursery so Teri could get some good uninterrupted sleep. And Leo had said...

She jerked her head around to the other side of her bed. He was there, sprawled in a chair, his head dropped onto his chest, eyes closed, fast asleep. A smile burst across her face. He hadn't left her side. He'd stayed to make sure no one woke her up, either intentionally or accidentally. The hospital staff had

178

steered him wrong last night and he wasn't about to be put off being right here for her today.

He was looking after her.

She relaxed onto her pillow and revelled in the pleasure of just looking at him. He was the loveliest man. His wavy black hair was mussed, lending an endearing, almost little-boy quality to his handsome face. Of course, his eyes changed that when they were open...such powerful, riveting, blue eyes. And his body was all man...the sexiest, most exciting body a woman could ever know and be pleasured by.

She was so lucky to have met him, even more lucky that he had come to love her. And it wasn't because he was gorgeous on the outside. What was inside was best of all...a caring, giving heart, lined up with a strength of character that didn't shy at anything that he considered had to be done. It was a wonderful feeling to have him at her side, ready to support and protect her.

There was a light tap on the door.

Leo snapped awake, his head instantly jerking up. He darted a sharp glance at the bed, caught her gaze on him, and his face relaxed into a sparkling grin. "Hi, new Mum!"

She grinned back. "Hi, new Dad!"

"You can come in," he called to the person at the door.

A nurse entered, smiling at Teri. "You've had a good sleep. Almost eight hours."

"Eight hours? Then it must be..."

"The 2:00 p.m. feed coming up and your little one needs to get started on it," the nurse said indulgently.

"But first, since you missed lunch, can I order something for you?"

"Tea and toast?" Teri asked, not really feeling hungry.

"Won't be long."

"Before you go, Nurse, could we have the baby in here?" she pressed hopefully. "I'd like to see her."

"I'll wheel her right in," the nurse promised and off she went.

Leo picked up a carrier bag from beside his chair and handed it to Teri, his eyes twinkling with happy anticipation. "Something I bought for you to wear in hospital."

"For *me*?"

She pulled out a lovely, soft, deep lavender-blue dressing gown in a light towelling fabric.

"I got Dylan's mother to sew the motifs on the pockets," Leo said eagerly. "She came by the hospital to give me the bag while you were asleep. Took a peep at our baby, too, and said to give you her congratulations."

It was her restaurant logo—the red heart with the white smile—sewn onto the pockets. A huge wave of emotion welled up and blurred her eyes with tears. She'd been so wrong about Leo not thinking of her, not buying her anything, not loving her. This lovely gift with the two happy hearts…he'd planned and arranged it especially for her, taking the time and effort to make it uniquely personal.

She took a deep breath and looked at him with her heart in her eyes. "I love it, Leo. Thank you so much. Not just for this. For everything you are to me."

She wished she had something to give him, to show him he was uniquely special to her, too, but all she could do was hold out her arms and hug him tight as they shared a kiss that encompassed a wealth of pleasure in their togetherness.

"Coming in…"

Their baby!

Leo broke away to grab the hospital bassinet from the nurse and roll it over to her bedside. He picked up the tidily wrapped white bundle from it and very carefully and gently transferred it to Teri's eagerly waiting arms. "She's still asleep," he whispered.

She looked down at a cute little feminine face framed by an unruly mass of black hair and her heart turned over. "She's so beautiful!" It was a sigh of sheer wonderment.

"She sure is," Leo warmly agreed, leaning over to drop a kiss on their daughter's head. "Absolutely perfect."

Teri glanced at the fatuous smile on his face and the word, *besotted*, came into her mind. "What will we call her, Leo?"

"You choose. You went through it all, giving birth to her."

His eyes eloquently retained the memory of her labour. Strangely enough, Teri could dismiss it now. It was over. Gone. And she had this beautiful baby girl…Leo's child.

"I want you to name her." It was something she could give him, the pleasure of his own choice.

"Well, I kind of like Lucy," he said slowly. He

shrugged and offered a whimsical smile. "Every time
I look at her I think…Lucy."

"Then Lucy it is. Lucy Kingston sounds great. You
could get the marriage forms on Monday, Leo," Teri
rushed on, remembering how keen he'd been on their
child having his name. "Lucy doesn't have to be registered for six weeks. We could get married before
then."

His face lit up. "You mean it?"

"Yes, I do. There's no need to book anywhere. We
could use a celebrant and have a wedding on the
beach at Bateau Bay and a fun party at my parents'
home afterwards. What do you think?" she cried eagerly.

Thank God for Mavis! he thought, making a swift
mental note to bring his trusty advisor to the hospital
to meet Teri and see their baby after he picked up the
marriage application forms on Monday.

"A wedding on the beach?" *Definitely not a register office.* "Great idea!" he said with such enthusiasm, the baby's eyes flicked open and the newly
named Lucy Kingston gazed wonderingly at her father.

Leo laughed. "Look at her, sizing me up."

Teri was absolutely certain Leo would always size
up fine in their daughter's eyes. *My darling daughter,*
she thought, remembering the card her parents had
sent on her thirtieth birthday.

"Did Mum and Dad say if they were coming to
visit when you phoned them?" she asked.

"They'll be here tonight. Dad and Donna, too."
Leo grinned. "They can't wait to see the new addition

to the family. Your brothers and their wives wanted to come, as well, but I told them tomorrow would be better. I thought everyone at once might be too much for you." His eyes flashed concern. "Was I right?"

"Yes. It would be far too crowded and noisy with all of them here together, though it's nice that they want to come."

"I got Dylan and Mel to stick a sign in the restaurant window for the customers, announcing It's A Girl! They're both going to buzz in to visit us this afternoon between the lunch and dinner shifts."

She laughed. "They're probably acting like new dads themselves." A thought suddenly struck her and she gazed with very clear eyes at the man who'd so totally changed her life. "You arranged everything, didn't you?"

"What?" He adopted an innocent look.

She smiled. "It's the champagne."

"Pardon?"

"The flowers, the visits, my happy heart dressing gown...you always were the champagne man."

His brow puckered. "I don't know what you're talking about, Teri."

"You, Leo. I'm talking about you."

She held out her hand, which he took, and a warm fizz ran up her arm. She wondered if Lucy felt a warm fizz, too, when her father cuddled her. The powerhouse of energy Leo stored in his heart probably radiated all over her. As it did with Teri.

"Until I met you, all my life was like an ordinary cup of tea," she explained. "Sometimes it had sugar in it. Sometimes..." her mouth momentarily turned down "...a slice of lemon."

He nodded, listening with an intensity that encouraged her to go on.

"You were like champagne, Leo. My first taste of it. And I loved it. Loved you for giving it to me. And I think now, that falling pregnant with Lucy wasn't an accident. It was the champagne having its way, creating the magic that made all this possible. And you just keep giving it to me...the wonderful, happy, bubbly feeling that makes everything beautifully right. Does that make sense to you?"

"Yes," he answered huskily. "It says it all. For me, too."

In one accord they both turned their gaze to the baby in her arms, the baby they'd made together.

Lucy looked up at them with big trusting eyes.

The miracle, the magic of having Leo's child, Teri thought.

A circle of love.

Complete.

If you enjoyed what you just read,
then we've got an offer you can't resist!

Take 2 bestselling
love stories FREE!

Plus get a FREE surprise gift!

HARLEQUIN®
Makes any time special ™

In celebration of Harlequin®'s golden anniversary

Enter to win a *dream!* You could win:

- A luxurious trip for two to *The Renaissance Cottonwoods Resort* in Scottsdale, Arizona, or

- A bouquet of flowers once a week for a year from **FTD**, or

- A $500 shopping spree, or

- A fabulous bath & body gift basket, including **K-tel**'s *Candlelight and Romance* 5-CD set.

Look for **WIN A DREAM** flash on specially marked Harlequin® titles by Penny Jordan, Dallas Schulze, Anne Stuart and Kristine Rolofson in October 1999*.

RENAISSANCE.
COTTONWOODS RESORT
SCOTTSDALE, ARIZONA

K-TEL

*No purchase necessary—for contest details send a self-addressed envelope to Harlequin Makes Any Time Special Contest, P.O. Box 9069, Buffalo, NY, 14269-9069 (include contest name on self-addressed envelope). Contest ends December 31, 1999. Open to U.S. and Canadian residents who are 18 or over. Void where prohibited.

PHMATS-GR

HARLEQUIN PRESENTS®

*invites you to see
how the other half marry in:*

SOCIETY WEDDINGS

This sensational new five-book miniseries invites
you to be our VIP guest at some of the most talked-
about weddings of the decade—spectacular events
where the cream of society gather to celebrate the
marriages of dazzling brides and grooms in
breathtaking, international locations.

Be there to toast each of the happy couples:

Aug. 1999—**The Wedding-Night Affair**, #2044,
Miranda Lee

Sept. 1999—**The Impatient Groom**, #2054,
Sara Wood

Oct. 1999—**The Mistress Bride**, #2056,
Michelle Reid

Nov. 1999—**The Society Groom**, #2066,
Mary Lyons

Dec. 1999—**A Convenient Bridegroom**, #2067,
Helen Bianchin

Available wherever Harlequin books are sold.

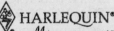

HARLEQUIN®
Makes any time special ™

Coming Next Month

HARLEQUIN PRESENTS®

THE BEST HAS JUST GOTTEN BETTER!